ORPHANAGE MISS

ORPHANAGE MISS

Clare Rossiter

Chivers Press
Bath, Avon, England

•

G.K. Hall & Co.
Thorndike, Maine USA

This Large Print edition is published by Chivers Press, England, and by G.K. Hall & Co., USA.

Published in 1996 in the U.K. by arrangement with the author.

Published in 1996 in the U.S. by arrangement with Laurence Pollinger Ltd.

U.K. Hardcover   ISBN   0–7451–3981–7 (Chivers Large Print)
U.K. Softcover   ISBN   0–7451–3993–0 (Camden Large Print)
U.S. Softcover   ISBN   0–7838–1623–5 (Nightingale Collection Edition)

The text of this Large Print edition is unabridged.
Other aspects of the book may vary from the original edition.

Set in 16 pt. New Times Roman.

Printed in Great Britain on acid-free paper.

British Library Cataloguing in Publication Data available

Library of Congress Cataloging-in-Publication Data

Rossiter, Clare.
  Orphanage miss / Clare Rossiter. — Large print ed.
    p.   cm.
  ISBN 0–7838–1623–5 (lg. print : lsc)
  1. Large type books.   I. Title.
[PS3568.O8473O77   1996]
813'.54—dc20   95–49321

CHAPTER ONE

The long journey from Portsmouth had been both tiring and hot. At first the passengers crowded together in the small interior of the coach and the unknown countryside passing by had interested her, but after a while nothing could distract from the discomforts of the hard seats and too little space allotted to each person. By the time Leahook was reached in the late afternoon, Amy Clear was glad to relinquish the small child who had occupied her lap for several miles to his mother and climb out into the fresh air of the yard of the Blue Anchor Inn.

Avoiding the bustling ostlers and hurrying grooms, she crossed the cobbled yard and went into the dim interior of the old building. The landlady, who was a kindly, if busy soul, swept her with a knowledgeable eye, taking in the untrimmed bonnet, the plain brown bombazine dress and coat and the worn portmanteau. Summing her up as a governess setting out for a new post and with little money to spare, she offered her a glass of lemonade in a small parlour and, calling a maid to escort her there, prepared to pass on to more important customers.

'My name is Clear,' said Amy quietly, pulling off her gloves and folding them. 'I am

1

to be met.'

'No one's asked for you yet, miss,' she was told, 'but I'll take note of the name.'

Amy followed the striped skirts of the trim serving-maid into the depths of the inn and was glad when the door of a small room was closed on her and she was left alone. A cool breeze blew in at a small window, and crossing the room she sat down in the window and gazed out. Washing was spread to dry on the hedges, bleaching in the sun, a small boy was busy in a vegetable patch and, nearer the house, a long flowerbed was an attraction for bees.

As she untied the long strings of her bonnet and placed it on the seat beside her, she could hear the pleasant sound of their humming. Loosening the tight bun that scraped back her light brown hair, she leaned her aching head against the window shutters and closed her eyes.

Immediately the room seemed to rock and sway with the motion of the coach she had so lately vacated and Amy opened her eyes hastily, just as the maid appeared with a glass of lemonade and a plate of ratafia biscuits.

Smiling her thanks and encouraged by the girl's obvious friendliness, she ventured to ask a question. 'Do you know a house near here called Kingsclear Court?'

'Yes 'm. Though 'tisn't near here. 'Tis a good few miles away. I've heard tell as it's as big as a palace!'

2

Amy's eyes widened. 'Really?' she said, trying to hide her surprise. 'I had not supposed it was anything out of the ordinary.'

The girl laughed. 'Kingsclear Court and Raven Hall in Hampshire stand above all,' she quoted as she left.

Sipping her drink thoughtfully, Amy stared at the sunlit garden beyond the window. Idly wondering about the unknown houses as the jingle danced in her head. 'Kingsclear,' she whispered. 'Kingsclear Court.'

It had been the name that had first attracted her attention. The paper was to have been used to light a fire and had somehow found its way into a school cupboard. Unable to resist the temptation, she had picked it up to read later. As her eyes travelled eagerly over the page, she had read that Sir William Kingsclear had met with a fatal accident in the hunting field and that he left a sorrowing widow and progeny. In fact she gathered the whole countryside was considerably shaken and shocked by his demise. That the late Sir William had been a gentleman of not inconsiderable virtues she was prepared to accept, but it was the name of his widow that held her interest.

Charlotte Kingsclear was a name that she had been brought up with, it being written boldly on the fly leaf of her bible, the only thing that she had brought with her to the genteel orphanage where she had spent most of her life.

3

Many had been the speculations and stories that she had woven around the unknown lady with the name so very near her own. When she was old enough she had asked who paid the fees for her upkeep and when told that it arrived each month from an unknown source, she had been sure that Charlotte was her benefactress and from that day on had faithfully included her in her prayers at night.

Only someone brought up in an orphanage without the benefit of relations would know the longing for a family, to belong to someone and, on sudden impulse, Amy had written to Lady Kingsclear, tentatively asking if there was any possibility of kinship between them. Almost at once, she had regretted the impulse and when a letter on heavy, expensive paper had arrived for her, she held it with trembling fingers, examining the seal, the franking on the back—anything rather than open it.

The letter had been a model of brevity, almost curt. Making no reference of relationship, it had stated that if Miss Clear would be at the Blue Anchor, Leahook on Wednesday of next week the coach would be met. The same bold signature that crossed her Bible, scrawled across the bottom of the page and, for the first time, Amy wondered at the reality behind the dream Charlotte Kingsclear that she had created.

The sound of the latch being lifted jerked her awake and she realised that she had fallen

4

asleep on the window-seat. Jumping to her feet, she faced the door, her heart beat quickening as she expected to meet the emissary from Kingsclear Court, but the substantial form of the landlady appeared in the opening.

'Will you be ordering dinner, if you please, miss,' she asked across the room that was filling with lengthening shadows as the sun began to leave the sky.

Suddenly Amy remembered the meagre breakfast which had been her last meal and realised how hungry she was. She hesitated, her mind flying to the few coins that had been left in her purse after paying for her ticket on the coach and at last answered reluctantly, 'I don't think I will bother, someone is sure to come soon.'

The landlady was not deceived, in her experience most governesses had thin purses. 'Sadie mentioned that you were asking after Kingsclear Court—will that be where you are staying, miss?' She went on at Amy's nod. 'Then let me offer you a plate of meat at no charge—we're always pleased to be of service to the Kingsclears.'

Amy stared after her retreating back, for the first time perceiving the deference paid to the aristocracy and rich, knowing that if she had been only an unknown governess on her way to a post, her treatment would most probably have been quite different.

She had barely finished her meal, when a

commotion in the yard made her hurry to the window on the other side of the room. A slender, high sprung carriage had just swept under the gate and, from the speed with which an ostler jumped to the horses' heads, she gathered that the person driving must be of some importance locally and transferred her gaze to the tall gentleman descending from his high perch.

She had time to notice white buckskin breeches and red regimentals crossed by the black triangle of an arm sling, before grey eyes were turned inquiringly in her direction and she looked away, backing hastily into the anonymity of the room.

A few minutes later, firm footsteps approached her retreat and, as though impelled, Amy stood up, one hand to her throat as, after a preliminary knock the door was opened.

She was surprised to see the soldier on the threshold; even the maid's words had failed to prepare her for the magnificence of the equipage that had been sent for her.

'Miss Clear?' the tall man demanded. 'I am Ellis Pensford. Lady Kingsclear has asked me to escort you to the Court.'

Wondering at the veiled hostility behind the curt words, Amy dropped into a slight curtsy and the last rays of the setting sun struck a halo from her smooth nut-brown hair.

'Good God!' exclaimed the man, much

6

struck by the effect. 'At least you have equipped yourself with the right coloured hair!' At her enquiring look, he explained rather begrudgingly, 'We all have red hair—of some kind.'

Her eyes flew to his glossy curls and she saw that indeed they were some kind of red; a dark auburn. Her heart beat an impatient tattoo against her high-waisted bodice, but before she could speak there was a timid tap at the door and Ellis Pensford strode across to jerk it open.

The diminutive maid stood in the passage holding a tray, containing cups and a steaming teapot, which the man eyed disparagingly.

'For the lady, sir,' she explained, glancing up at him, her eyes wide with obvious admiration. 'Mr Jones wondered as if you'd care for something stronger, Captain?'

'Indeed I would,' he said, taking the tray from her and balancing it dextrously with his one free hand. 'Fetch me a mug of ale, like a good girl.'

'You have been well looked after?' he asked Amy perfunctorily, setting the tray on a small table.

'Oh, yes,' she answered demurely, 'I've had time to refresh myself.'

He gave a short laugh. 'You mean you've been waiting rather longer than you like.' He moved closer, looking down at her from his greater height. 'Take my advice, Miss Clear, or whatever your name is, and give up this wild

7

scheme now, before you regret it—'

He broke off abruptly as the maid entered and swung away to seat himself on one of the window-seats. Amy busied herself with the tray, trying to appear calm and still the trembling of her hands, as she poured the tea. When they were alone again, a tense silence grew in the room, the Captain sipping his drink as he eyed her and Amy stirring her tea with restless fingers, well aware of his gaze.

'I—really have no idea what you mean,' she said at last, almost conversationally, when it was obvious that he intended to make her speak first.

He moved abruptly. 'Oh, come now,' he said harshly. 'You saw the notice of Sir William's death in the paper, realised that his widow would be in the throes of grief and decided upon this masquerade—this charade. I grant you that your letter was a masterpiece of understatement and innuendo—but believe me you have no hope of obtaining anything from Lady Kingsclear. She is a very astute woman and will not be swayed by any of your intentions to play on her feelings . . . and even if she were not, you would still have me to deal with.'

Feeling almost physically attacked, Amy gazed at him, her brown eyes wide with astonishment. 'Wh-what do you mean?' she gasped, 'I don't know what you are talking about!' Setting her cup back in its saucer with

8

sudden resolution, she stood up. 'If in fact you have been truly sent to convey me to Kingsclear Court, which let me tell you I begin to doubt, for you seem more like a madman than anyone sent upon an errand, then I suggest you do so.'

He leaned back against the shutters and surveyed her from behind half closed lids. 'How much do you set upon this game?' he asked slowly and, reaching into an inside pocket, pulled out a purse and tossed it on the table by her side. 'There's a hundred guineas— take it and I'll tell my aunt that no one got off the Portsmouth coach.'

Amy stared at him in growing bewilderment, feeling her ready temper begin to rise. 'I have no idea who you might be,' she told him indignantly, 'or why you should feel called upon to insult me, but let me tell you, sir, that I am determined to see Lady Kingsclear and visit her I will, whether I have to hire a carriage or walk.'

Her own determination surprised her and she put the thought of her empty purse away with resolution, suddenly realising that this unexpected opposition had only served to make her wish more dearly to see the mysterious Charlotte Kingsclear.

The soldier, who had been watching her keenly, reached out a brown hand. 'Come here,' he commanded.

Amy looked at him sharply, lifting her chin

9

a little.

'Come into the light, where I can see you.'

His voice held the tone of one used to command and before she realised what was happening, to her chagrin her feet carried her forward. Taking her wrist, he drew her a little nearer, turning her so that the last rays of sun would fall on her face. Although she was dazzled by the light, she knew that his grey eyes were travelling over her and a warm flush coloured her cheeks. Biting her lip, she gazed over his head out at the garden that was slowly growing grey with dusk.

At last he released her and she turned away, rubbing her wrist where his long fingers had held her.

'You're one of us,' he admitted, reluctantly. 'You have all the looks of a Kingsclear.'

He was unprepared for the blaze of pleasure that glowed in her eyes and his own gaze suddenly sharpened as his black brows drew together in a quick frown.

'A Kingsclear,' whispered Amy, seeming unaware of his presence or of his intent gaze as he watched her face.

'A natural child—a love child. Your parents'll not have had the blessings of the clergy,' he told her, harshly.

She flushed as much at the fact that he used such blunt terms to her as at his tone and turned her brilliant eyes towards him. 'What does that matter?' she asked quietly. 'I dare say

10

that to you it's of great import, but to me it means very little. If you had spent all your life in an orphanage, with no one of your own—not a single person to care whether you lived or died, you would know how I feel. To find that I have a family—however tenuous the link—is above all wonderful to me.'

He watched her thoughtfully. 'You are either clever or very naïve, Miss Clear,' he commented lazily. 'I'm not sure which.' Abruptly he stood up, towering over her. 'I'll take you to the Court,' he said unexpectedly. 'I believe you might distract my aunt and, at the moment, that is what she needs—but be very sure I will remove you at the first sign of your disrupting the family or upsetting her.'

He seemed very large and menacing as he uttered his soft voiced warning and Amy felt chill fingers of fear slide down her back. She shivered involuntarily as she picked up her bonnet and tied the ribbons under her chin.

'I have no wish to disturb anyone—but to find someone of my own would be beyond all things,' she told him quietly, her tone so unconsciously wistful that Captain Pensford's rather hard features softened momentarily.

Taking her arm, he called for someone to bring her baggage and seemed considerably surprised when she pointed out her single piece of luggage.

'Do you intend to stay only over night?' he asked blankly.

11

A painful flush flew to Amy's cheeks. 'As a teacher in an orphanage, I haven't need for much,' she said, hanging her head.

Grey eyes travelled over the ugly bonnet, its deep brim almost hiding its wearer's face, examined the plain, worn brown dress and coat and stopped on the girl's thin hand, twisting a pair of neatly darned gloves between agitated fingers.

'Just so,' he said slowly. 'I like to travel light, myself.'

Amy's eyes flew to his face at the unexpected kindness, but he was turning away to settle the reckoning and, a moment later, she was swept out of the inn to where the carriage waited in the cobbled yard.

She hung back a little, but when she was handed up into the high seat, she made no demur, not wishing to make known her fear of horses. The Captain seated himself beside her, the groom sprang up behind and they swept out of the yard in a flurry of movement and noise.

Amy noticed that Ellis Pensford seemed able to control his matched greys with tolerable skill despite having one arm incommoded by some injury. He turned his head to look down at her and caught her eyes upon his sling.

'I see you have been wounded,' she felt constrained to say.

'A scratch from a French bullet,' he told her briefly. 'The doctors tell me that it will mend in

12

time, but it's put an end to my soldiering at the moment. I've just been to the War Office to resign my commission.'

'Do you mind?'

He glanced down at her, gave his attention back to the horses as he tooled them round a tight corner and then spoke. 'I've spent the last ten years fighting on the Continent—I began to feel that I've had enough of war.'

'Living in Portsmouth we see the bands and regiments marching to embark on the ships. It's a brave sight, but there's nothing gay about the ships filled with sick and wounded, or the maimed soldiers begging in the streets.'

'True, Miss Clear, I had not supposed you so perceptive.'

'I fail to see why being an orphan, or wishing to get in touch with my possible relatives, should make me devoid of feelings in your opinion.'

'In my opinion, Miss Clear, you would have shown better sensibility by not intruding upon a family in mourning.'

'Sir William's death occurred some time ago. I imagined that Lady Kingsclear would be over the first flush of grief,' she excused herself.

'I suppose the amount of grief felt, would depend upon the depths of feeling given to the deceased person,' he pointed out dryly.

'And Lady Kingsclear was very fond of her husband?'

He didn't answer her question, merely

13

contenting himself by pointing out several interesting landmarks that could just be discerned in the gathering dusk.

Amy shivered in her thin coat, feeling the evening damp settling about her.

'There's a rug on the seat beside you,' said her companion without taking his eyes from the road ahead.

Pulling the rug around her knees and tucking her cold hands into its soft folds, warmth soon returned to the girl and she could give her attention to the countryside around them.

The dusty road shone white in the dim light, like a ribbon being devoured by the steady feet of the greys. A range of hills hung dim and misty, a few miles away to the right, while rich fields of corn and pasture crowded close on either side of the road. Clumps of tall trees broke up the landscape and gradually grew thicker until dense woods seemed to be advancing towards them.

'Do—we drive through the trees?' she asked in a small voice.

Ellis Pensford shot her an amused glance. 'Afraid of highwaymen, Miss Clear?' he asked wickedly. 'Or perhaps it's ghosts and bogies that are your especial fear.'

'I daresay a country girl would be afraid of a town at night,' she pointed out reasonably, the rug hiding her hands clenched together in her lap. 'I, Captain Pensford, have never been out

14

in the country at night, you must make allowances for my vapours—I shall endeavour not to have a screaming spasm!'

'I would strongly advise against such a thing—the horses would undoubtedly take fright and upset us. However, in case of a High Tobyman appearing, if you could manage to lean a little to the left, John behind, who is armed with a pistol, will make an effort to shoot between us.'

Amy's bosom heaved with indignation, the more so as she heard a chuckle from behind and knew that the groom had heard every word of their exchange.

'I am persuaded that you are joking,' she said in a stifled voice, trying not to notice the dark shadows between the trees that could hide any amount of robbers or watchful spirits.

Suddenly the man behind made a movement and from the corner of her eyes Amy could see that he had brought out a long, thin trumpet.

'Take care,' warned Captain Pensford, 'John is about to wake up the occupants of the lodge in the hopes that the gates will be open by the time we get there.'

An ear-splitting shriek shattered the cool night and involuntarily the girl's hands flew to cover her ears. The carriage made a wide swing to the left, Amy had a vague impression of a small house huddled to one side and of a boy with a lantern standing by a wide gate and then

15

they were through two stone pillars and trotting along a sweeping driveway.

The moon had risen and turned the still waters of a large ornamental lake to silver, silhouetting huge trees against the smooth undulating parkland.

Amy caught her breath, a feeling, almost indescribable filled her with a sense of home-coming and she was unable to conceal her obvious delight from the cynical gaze of her companion.

'Better than you expected, Miss Clear?'

Glancing at him impatiently, she hunched a shoulder, unwilling to be distracted from the task of drinking in the surroundings that held so much attraction for her. 'The drive swings round just ahead,' she said quietly, 'and the house is just behind the trees, overlooking the lake.'

For a moment there was silence. 'Very clever,' murmured Ellis Pensford. 'You must have been here before or known someone who has—it would not be difficult.'

'No,' she protested, bewildered herself at her unexpected knowledge and her heart fluttered strangely, when a few minutes later her description was proved true.

A dark mass of buildings loomed up with sharp, finger-like chimneys jutting against the deep blue night sky. The chaise stopped beside a shallow flight of steps and a wide door was flung open as Captain Pensford handed the reins to his groom and swung down to the gravelled drive.

Amy accepted his hand and climbed nimbly down from the high seat, her eyes wide as she stared up at the huge, towering house. Ellis took her elbow in a firm grip and, feeling not unlike a prisoner being led into captivity, she was escorted to the front door.

'This is Miss Clear,' he said to the aged man who waited with a candelabra held above his head. 'Wilkins,' he explained briefly to Amy, 'is Lady Kingsclear's butler—I leave you in his safe hands.'

Nodding curtly, he let go her arm and ran lightly down the steps to his carriage. Feeling strangely lost, the girl gazed after him, before turning to the waiting butler.

'Captain Pensford does not live here?'

'No, Miss. The Captain resides at Raven Hall. His land meets ours on the west side of the park.'

'I see—' While the butler closed the door, Amy looked round the great hall in which she found herself, the candles sent flickering light over the checkered floor, while the ceiling and distant corners were hidden in black shadows.

'We keep early hours here, miss. My lady left word that she will see you after breakfast in the morning.'

Wilkins lifted the branch of candles and started towards the staircase that led upwards in a shallow curve from one end of the square hall. As the flames flared in a sudden draft Amy became aware that a dim figure was leaning over the banisters, peering down at her. For a moment, shadowed, cavernous eyes met hers, then, in a swirl of white drapery, the figure was gone ... and the old retainer was glancing back curiously at Amy's startled gasp.

'There was someone looking down—'

'The family have all retired,' he said repressively, continuing to mount the stairs steadily so that she was forced to follow the pool of light, unless she wished to be left in the dark.

'Someone in white—'

'You must be mistaken, miss,' the butler said firmly and, having reached the head of the stairs, turned under a high arch and marched along a wide corridor.

'I'll send a maid to you, miss,' he said, opening a door and standing aside for her to enter.

The door closed silently behind her and Amy was almost inclined to call him back, before she took in the fact that the candles on the mantelpiece lit a very pleasant room and felt her nervous fears begin to subside; her arrival, the dark house and aged manservant had brought to mind very vividly the circumstances and plot of the latest 'Gothic' novel she had read. Coupled with her lack of welcome, absence of her hostess and the sight of the white figure on the stairs, these facts had filled her with alarm and she had begun to wonder in what kind of household she was to find herself.

However the sight of the very ordinary room, which was more comfortable and luxurious than any she had ever imagined, soothed her fears and she was able to remove her bonnet and cross to the dressing table with tolerable calm. The swinging mirror showed her a pale face and two huge anxious eyes surveying her reflection with obvious apprehension as she wondered nervously what the morrow would bring.

Almost she wished she had not written the fateful letter, but then her natural courage rose to her rescue and, taking new heart, she had to admit that a sense of excitement filled her at the thought of what the future might hold.

CHAPTER TWO

The maid, who had brought refreshments and a can of hot water, had only just left when, after a light tap, the door opened again and a girl in a blue wrap entered quickly.

Pale hair that only just escaped the description of being ginger, rioted in curls and waves over her shoulders as she smiled at Amy and touched her lips in a gesture of conspiracy that told the other girl to speak in whispers.

'I had to come and welcome you,' she

breathed. 'I've waited all day to see your arrival—it's too bad of Ellis to take so long in London.' Smiling, she held out a hand. 'You must be Amy Clear. I'm Lydia Brent—Lyddie, usually.'

'How do you do,' said the other girl politely.

'I see you've been left a tray—shall I pour some tea for you and then we can sit by the window and talk. That is, if you would like to, of course.'

'I ... think I'd like that very much,' said Amy, suddenly warming to this unknown girl who had stayed up to welcome her.

'Did you have a pleasant journey?' asked Lyddie as they seated themselves on the window-seat overlooking the moonlit garden.

'It was very hot and uncomfortable, but I found it interesting, never having left Portsmouth before.'

'Did you have a companion?'

Amy realised that the other was asking discreetly if she had a maid and smiled slightly. 'I travelled on the stage by myself,' she explained rather proud of her achievement.

'Goodness!' gasped Lyddie, her eyes round with astonishment. 'How brave!'

'Orphanages don't run to maidservants,' Amy told her dryly.

'Of course not, how stupid of me, but weren't you nervous?'

Amy shook her head. 'Not until Captain Pensford handed me up into his carriage. I'd never been so near horses before and the seat seemed so flimsy and the ground so far below!'

The other girl laughed. 'I assure you that with Ellis you were in good hands. He's a first class whip.'

Silence fell between them and Amy saw that Lydia was examining her covertly, at last she reached forward and touched the thick plait of hair that hung over Amy's shoulder.

'I see that you have the Kingsclear hair,' she said gently. 'In me it's been diluted into this dreadful sandy colour and Medora has missed it all together.'

'So Captain Pensford told me—'

'Forgive me for asking—but are you one of us? With that hair and a name like Clear, it seems more than likely.'

Amy stood up and crossed the room to stand in front of the dressing-table watching her companion in the mirror. 'I—don't know,' she told her honestly. 'Captain Pensford seems to think me some kind of adventuress, intent upon foistering myself upon Lady Kingsclear, but really I have no intention of doing such a thing.' Suddenly she turned to face Lydia, speaking frankly and impulsively. 'You see, I've lived with her name all my life—made stories about her, pretended she was my mother and when I found out that she was a real person, I couldn't resist the chance to get in touch with her.'

Lyddie's blue eyes were wide circles of

21

excitement and interest. 'It's like a novel,' she breathed. 'Were you a foundling, with a locket of hair pinned to your dress? Amy—tell me all.'

Never having had such an enthralled listener, Amy was very happy to oblige and soon Lyddie knew all her early history.

'Oh, how dreadful,' she cried sympathetically, obviously understanding the feelings of the other girl. 'And what happened when the money for the fees ceased?'

'The Governors decided, after attempting to find my benefactor, that I could stay on provided as soon as I was old enough, I would take an unpaid post at the orphanage for five years, which I did ... but for the last two years I have been paid £10 per annum.'

Amy felt justifiably proud of her value, but Lyddie's face was a mixture of emotions at the knowledge that someone could be paid, for working long and arduous hours, less than half the pin-money she was allowed herself.

'Were you happy?' she asked curiously.

'Happy? I hardly know. Most times I was too busy to be other than tired, but I suppose I wasn't unhappy—not all the time anyway. Although strict, the regime wasn't unduly harsh ... we were never allowed to forget that we were gentlefolk and had to behave as ladies at all times. As a child I remember running across the yard one day and having to face into a corner all the afternoon, while the others walked along the seawalls. I expect your governess was just as strict.'

Lydia agreed uncertainly, remembering the many kindly ladies who had endeavoured to instil learning into herself and her sister, until suddenly recalling the lateness of the hour, she stood up, preparing to return to her own chamber.

'Was it you I saw on the stairs when I came?' asked Amy, remembering the silent figure hanging over the banisters.

'No,' said Lyddie positively. 'I was watching from the window. It might have been Medora.'

'Medora?'

'*My* sister. What did she look like?'

'I could hardly see, but she was wearing soft white robes of some kind.'

Lydia stared at her curiously. 'On the stairs, you say? Good Lord!' She suddenly exclaimed, much struck by a new idea. 'I hope you didn't mention it to Wilkins.'

'I did as it happens and he seemed quite determined that I was mistaken and that there was no one there.'

'I expect he believes you've seen the White Nun.'

'I had thought that Kingsclear was a private house. Are you telling me that it's a nunnery?'

'Not now—but years ago it was. A long time ago it was dissolved and the inmates dispersed, but one was left behind ... so the story goes.'

Amy looked at her, her mouth a little open on a quivering breath. 'You mean a—ghost?'

In spite of her commonsense, a cold shiver ran down her spine as she recalled the silent watching figure. 'I'd liefer far believe it was your sister, Medora,' she said hopefully.

'It would be like her,' agreed Lyddie thoughtfully. 'She's very curious about you.' She paused awkwardly and then went on in an embarrassed voice. 'She—can be a little difficult. I'm afraid that after Mama died she was spoilt and is used to finding herself the centre of interest. If you take attention away from her she might be a little—unfriendly, I'm afraid.'

And so Amy was not unprepared for her reception when next morning she entered the breakfast room. Medora raised her eyebrows insolently and bowed ungraciously across the table as her sister introduced the newcomer.

Amy felt dazzled and cast into insignificance by her beauty. Golden curls framed a piquant face and huge, violet eyes looked out on the world with avarice not many suspected.

'Come and meet Grandmama's little foundling,' she called as a slim, fashionably dressed man strolled into the room.

Amy dropped into a curtsy and found her hand taken in a warm grasp. 'Denvil Martin—at your service,' said the man bowing elegantly and Amy felt her heart give a strange lurch as she looked up and encountered a pair of smiling blue eyes. 'We have all been in a fever of anxiety to meet Grandmama's new guest—had I known that she would be one so charming, I would have been even more impatient!' he went on gallantly.

Ignoring Medora's derisive snort from behind, Amy dimpled up at the gentleman grateful for his flattery, even though her commonsense told her that her unbecoming gown and hair style could only appear to disadvantage against the delicate dresses and glossy curls of the two sisters.

It had taken her one glance to know that her own wardrobe was quite inadequate and that against the others she must appear a poor, unfashionable dowd. Her heart sank as she mentally reviewed the amount in her slender purse and came to the conclusion that she could not hope to even purchase a ribbon or trinket to brighten her sombre gown, none the less, she took her seat at the breakfast table with a show of calm, accepted tea and toast and endeavoured to appear unconcerned by Medora's sharp gaze.

'She reminds me of that governess we had once,' she said suddenly to Lydia, speaking as though Amy were either deaf or not there. 'Do you remember? She had just that colour hair and that missish expression.'

Lyddie appeared uncomfortable, shooting Amy conciliatory glances and trying to quieten her sister.

'An I recall aright,' put in Denvil Martin quietly, 'she was the only one of a long succession to get the better of you, Medora.'

Amy smiled gratefully, while the fair girl subsided into an angry silence. Lyddie and Denvil talked of trivialities, drawing Amy into their conversation, until by the end of the meal, she was feeling more at ease and able to accept the summons to wait on Lady Kingsclear with outward composure, though her heart was beating uncomfortably fast as she followed the bent back of Wilkins as he led her to the lady's chamber.

Amy paused on the threshold as the butler announced her name, met by such an opulence of furnishings, soft muslins and shiny satins, that she was quite bewildered by such an array. Although the hour was advanced, the curtains were still half drawn and the plump lady reclining on a day-bed was wrapped in the voluminous folds of a pink négligée.

'Come in, child,' she ordered, 'and stand where I can see you.'

Amy found herself the object of a scrutiny from a pair of faded, blue eyes, almost hidden under a lacy cap, becomingly arranged over a mass of soft grey curls. Suddenly the lady's expression, which until then had only shown mild curiosity, altered and she gestured for someone behind her to open a curtain. As a shaft of sunlight struck Amy's hair, she heard the older woman catch her breath and allowed her own gaze to widen a little in inquiry.

'I told you she had the hair,' said a familiar

voice from the window embrasure and Amy looked up sharply to meet the faintly mocking eyes of Captain Pensford. Returning her slight curtsy with an even curter nod, he strolled forward. 'I think we'll have to admit that she's a Kingsclear,' he said.

'I never doubted it,' said Lady Kingsclear and held out her hand to the girl. 'Come closer and let me look at you.' Pulling Amy to kneel beside the couch, she studied her face for a few minutes before releasing her, she turned away, touching her eyes with the corner of a lace-edged handkerchief. 'Once, long ago,' she murmured, 'I knew someone very like you ... and held him dear.' Turning back to Amy, she patted her hand, motioning for her to stand up. 'Tell me all you know about yourself,' she said.

Amy stood uncertainly, until Ellis Pensford placed a chair for her beside the day-bed and retired to the fireplace, where he folded his arms and leaned his shoulder against the mantelpiece, watching her intently. Only too aware of his sardonic gaze, she avoided his eyes, looking instead at the lady, leaning against the piled cushions and clutching a bottle of smelling salts like a talisman.

'There is very little to tell,' she began after a while, her clear voice carrying across the silent room. She hesitated, seeking for words and then, taking a deep breath plunged into her story, telling it boldly, not looking for sympathy.

'And ... you remember nothing of your former life?'

'A little perhaps ... I remember a lady, whom I think must have been my mother, crying—but mostly I recall that once I was happy and then I—was not.' She raised her eyes and looked directly at the man by the fire. 'Last night I thought I remembered the drive and the house, but now I am not sure. I think I may have been told about it. Like a story.'

Lady Kingsclear made a sudden movement and Amy saw a tear escape and slide down her powdered cheek. A plump, beringed, hand reached out and touched her own. 'You shall stay here—'

'Madam, I beg of you consider clearly before you make a decision.' Ellis Pensford's clear voice cut across the woman's trembling tones. 'I pray you don't begin something that has no end.'

Her ladyship sent him a glance full of meaning. 'I am merely inviting Miss Clear to stay at the Park for a while,' she said. 'I assure you I have made no decision—as yet. If she pleases me ... things might be different.' She eyed Amy's clothes, not deigning to hide her disapproval. 'You'll need a new wardrobe,' she declared. 'I know you'll have more sense than to be annoyed that I say so. I'll see that the girls arrange it for you.'

Amy took a long, shuddering breath. 'Ma'am,' she began. 'I would be pleased to stay

28

here and honoured that you should ask me, but I must know the circumstances of your offer. Am I to have a position?'

Lady Kingsclear's mouth pursed thoughtfully as she considered.

'She's right Aunt Charlie,' the Captain admitted. 'We must think of something to quell gossip.'

'Once she is suitably attired, we shall let it be known that a distant cousin is paying us a visit,' declaimed the lady. She patted Amy's hand. 'The girls give me a little help with my letters and so on—you can do the same.' She smiled roguishly at her tall nephew. 'Ellis, an I remember rightly the Green Walk is just the place for a stroll on such a morning as this. Do you take your new cousin there and—become better acquainted.'

The soldier did not look best pleased, but he eased his shoulders away from the mantle and offered his arm to Amy.

The girl rose to her feet and looked from one to the other, with wide, bewildered eyes. 'But—I thought I would learn—That you would tell me who I was,' she whispered.

The pale blue eyes opened under the frivolous cap as Lady Kingsclear stared at Amy, then the lids lowered, veiling her gaze and she looked away. 'For the moment you must be content to be Amy Clear,' she said. 'Old memories, old troubles are too painful to be dredged up needlessly...'

Her voice wavered and Amy swung towards Ellis with a hopeless little gesture and found her fingers taken in a firm grip. Her hand was pulled under his elbow and, somehow, they were out of the dim bedchamber and she was being hurried along dark passages and down steep stairs until a door was opened and a blaze of sunlight almost blinded her.

'No!' she cried, screwing up her eyes and trying to tug free. 'I must go back—you don't understand—'

'Indeed, I do. You have plagued her ladyship enough.'

'Plagued!' she repeated indignantly. 'I hardly had chance to say a word. I came here hoping to learn who I was ... and all that happens is that I hear talk of someone whom I resemble, I am invited here to stay and none of my questions are answered at all.'

He looked down at her as she bit her lip. 'Be thankful for that,' he advised. 'You have done very well to be accepted into the house so easily.'

She stamped her foot. 'You say yourself that I am one of you,' she pointed out. 'You all think that I am a Kingsclear, but won't tell me who. Why? What has my father done to merit such mystery?'

'You would have done well to make inquiries before you set out upon this adventure,' he told her. 'Think how much better your position would be if you could have laid claim to a particular member of the family.'

'You are impossible!' she said in a stifled voice as Ellis Pensford tightened his grip on her reluctant fingers and began to lead her towards a stretch of smooth, green lawn.

'I am persuaded that you are not one of these delicate females who will feel called upon to swoon at the prospect of being out of doors without the protection of a bonnet and parasol,' he said blandly, suiting his long strides to her shorter steps. 'But we were talking about the more disreputable Kingsclears ... I believe there were several younger sons that were considered rather wild ... Uncle William himself was not above a wild oat or two, I believe. And ... some years ago the Kingsclears' young son made an unfortunate—alliance—and was dismissed the house and disowned by his father. He died not long after in a riding accident without being reconciled to his family.'

'And you think I might be his child?'

Captain Pensford glanced down. 'My dear Miss Clear, the choice is yours,' he answered lazily. 'On the other hand, and I own that this is the theory to which I incline, the Kingsclears have ever been profligate—red hair is exceedingly common among the local villages. I believe 'tis vulgarly termed the "Kingsclear Banner".'

He smiled coolly into her astounded face,

31

tightening his grasp a little when she would have pulled away. 'Don't run away,' he told her. 'We were enjoined to become better aquainted and I intend to do precisely that.'

'I ... believe that I have no wish for your better acquaintance,' said Amy coldly, lifting her chin a little.

'You would be wise not to assign me the part of your enemy,' he said quietly, his grey eyes narrow and menacing. He let his words hang between them before leading her forward again, he strolled gently along a cool green path shielded from the bright sun by thick foliaged trees. 'Let us examine the ruins,' he suggested, 'and while I gainsay to implant a little ancient history, you may tell me all the items you forgot to tell my aunt.'

Amy's heart beat quickened at the thought of an interrogation from the alarming man beside her and she waited in some suspense for his questions, but none came. Instead she was led under a small stone arch and into a ruined quadrangle, its four walls open to the sky and the high, pointed windows stark and empty. Grass covered what must have once been the floor, giving the impression of a lush, green carpet. Broken cloisters let off to one side, their slender arches and colonnades still beautiful as they shone white in the bright sunlight.

'The White Ladies lived here,' Ellis Pensford told her, 'until King Henry dissolved the Nunnery. He gave their land to a Kingsclear who happened to be in favour at the time. I believe the stone from the old religious house came in very useful when he began building his new home!'

'Lydia said something about a White Nun—' the girl began tentatively.

'All old houses have their ghost stories,' he said repressively. 'You, cousin Amy, would do well not to believe all that you hear.'

Amy looked up quickly, startled by his form of address and warned by an underlying meaning in his words that the conversation was about to take a new direction.

'And with that principle firmly in mind,' he went on, leading her towards a seat against a hedge, 'I would like to hear about your early life ... or as much as you are prepared to tell me.'

'I have already told you all there is,' said Amy, sinking onto the stone seat. 'I have led a very unadventurous life, I assure you. I was not left on the orphanage steps as a baby, neither was I found in a church, or stolen by gipsies.'

He sat beside her, leaning forward to watch her face and shield her from the sun. 'I am more interested in your adult life—If we eliminate all that you are not, we might be left with what you are,' he said lazily and possessed himself of one of her hands, examining her slender fingers and smooth skin. 'Neither are you a seamstress or kitchen wench.'

Amy forced herself to allow her hand to lie passively in his grasp. 'Doubtless you'll recall that I said I taught at the orphanage,' she reminded him quietly. 'May I suggest that you send a man to make enquiries there?'

'Already done,' he told her and watched intently for some sign of discomfiture or loss of assurance.

'Then you will only learn that I spoke the truth.'

'In so far as that you were an inmate of the Asylum for Gentlewomen—I'm afraid Miss Clear that you will still have a long way to go to convince me of your bona fides.'

Amy's dark eyes flashed and she widened her gaze at him. 'But, Captain Pensford,' she said sweetly, 'I understood that it was Lady Kingsclear that I had to convince!'

'Battle positions, Miss Clear?' she was asked as he, at last, released her hand and she was surprised to see a gleam of amusement at the back of his cold gaze.

'Let us say, that I found out at an early age that I had no one to fight my battles for me. As a small child I learned not to cry for what I wanted ... but to fight for it.'

Ellis Pensford had a momentary picture of a small indomitable girl with red hair, hiding her tears and determination and for a moment his hard expression softened slightly.

'You'll not frighten me away, Captain Pensford,' Amy went on decidedly, unconsciously bracing her slim shoulders. 'I've learned a certain indifference to hurts and insults and have every intention of finding out my true identity—perhaps then, I might decide to leave Kingsclear Park, but not until then.'

She deliberately held his eyes for a second, before standing up and shaking out her narrow skirts preparatory to walking away.

Ellis Pensford eyed her flushed cheeks and angry, sparkling eyes, with interest in his own grey glance. 'I thought I had brought home a small, brown sparrow,' he commented slowly, 'but find I've captured a fierce little bird, instead.'

Amy glared at him stormily and brushed her hand disparagingly over her dismal brown gown. 'These clothes are not of my choosing,' she snapped. 'They are what are considered suitable for an orphanage governess.'

'I had not supposed them actually chosen,' the Captain assured her, 'but rather to have happened by accident.'

Amy whisked on her heels and would have left him, but found that she had lost the direction of the house and had to accept his escort across the park. She found Lyddie waiting for her and was taken upstairs to the girl's sitting room.

'Grandmama says we are to lend you anything you need and tomorrow we will drive into town to make arrangements with Mrs Mulchett, our mantua-maker to set you up

35

with a summer wardrobe,' she told Amy.

'How kind of her,' exclaimed Amy, feeling a thrill of excitement at the thought of choosing new clothes.

'I thought—' went on Lyddie diffidently, 'that you might be persuaded to borrow a gown for dinner tonight—that is if you have brought nothing suitable with you.'

Medora, who had been reading a novel and ostentatiously ignoring Amy, dropped the book into her lap and yawned. 'There's the bundle of things I have no further use for and had put out for the servants,' she suggested languidly. 'You might find something in that.'

The other girl stiffened and lifted her head. 'I have no wish to borrow anything,' she retorted coldly. 'I have another gown with me—if it's not considered suitable, then I will dine in my room.' She turned on her heel and left the room in a swirl of anger, only to hear a scurry of footsteps and to feel Lyddie's hand on her arm, before she reached her own chamber.

'Amy—please don't be angry,' she pleaded. 'You must forgive her—truly she is having a trying time.' Drawing the other girl into the shelter of her bedroom, she lowered her voice and went on conspiratorily. 'Medora made an unfortunate alliance in London last season and Papa has sent her down here to Grandmama to forget the young man.'

Amy's thin eyebrows lifted. 'It would seem to be a failing in your family,' she

36

commented dryly.

Lydia looked puzzled for a moment, then her brow cleared. 'You mean Grandpapa,' she said, 'though we are supposed to know nothing of his failings.'

'I believe that red hair predominates in the local villages.'

'Well, the Kingsclears have been here for centuries,' supplied Lyddie candidly, before looking at her anxiously. 'You will come down to dinner, won't you? We'll dine en famille—only we and Ellis will be there.'

'What further inducement could I need?'

She looked up. 'Don't you like him? I know he can be a little formidable, but I can't think of anyone I'd leifer go to if I was in a scrape.'

Amy looked thoughtful at this new aspect of Captain Pensford. 'He believes me an adventuress,' she said boldly and turned away to bring her good dress out of the clothes-press and display it for Lyddie's inspection.

Thin grey cotton with a tiny silk spot had seemed eminently suitable for any important function at the orphanage, but she could clearly see that its use at Kingsclear Park would be sadly limited.

'Well—we are all in half mourning still for Grandpapa,' Lydia told her, 'so the colour is quite suitable. If you would allow me to lend you a lace tucker to wear over it, it would do very well.' She smiled hopefully at Amy. 'Do let me—no one would ever know and I would be very pleased to help you.'

She brightened at once when the other accepted her offer and ran off to her room to return almost at once with the white cotton 'front' that could be tied like a bib over a dress and so alter its appearance.

Amy thanked her and then asked her to explain the relationship of the members of the family. 'Captain Pensford calls Lady Kingsclear "aunt", but I am unsure what kinship is Mr Martin?'

'Denvil is our cousin, our mothers were half sisters. Grandmama married twice, you see. And Ellis's mother was Grandpapa's younger sister—I suppose he's a second cousin.'

When she had left the room, Amy tried the effect of the tucker against her sober gown and was rather pleased to see how the white cotton relieved the dull colour, making her skin, which she usually regarded as sallow, appear quite a pleasant shade of cream. She thought of the forthcoming dinner with some trepidation, nothing at the asylum had prepared her for life at Kingsclear Court and she was beginning to understand how precarious her position was.

Only Lydia and perhaps Denvil Martin were prepared to accept her presence with any feeling of friendliness ... both Ellis Pensford and Medora Brent made no pretence at anything but emnity. Her life at the orphanage had been tedious and dull, but quite suddenly it began to seem safe and secure compared to the tight-rope she seemed to be walking in this luxurious and comfortable house.

CHAPTER THREE

Early after luncheon the next day, the younger ladies of the Court set out in an open carriage for the little town of Leahook, under the watchful eye of an elderly female in a severe black gown and bonnet.

'This is Jessie Green, Grandmama's maid,' explained Lyddie as she seated herself on the wide seat beside her sister. 'Jessie, this is Miss Clear who is to be our guest for a while.'

'Yes, miss, her ladyship explained the circumstances.'

Amy turned her head at the enigmatic tones to look at the woman next to her and as she did so saw the other's expression alter as surprise showed for a moment in her eyes.

'M'lady said as you were kin, miss, but I can see that for myself.'

She would have said more, but Medora made an impatient gesture to the driver and the older woman seemed to recollect herself and compressed her lips as the carriage slid smoothly forward.

Lyddie and Medora put up parasols to shade their complexions, but Amy had to rely for protection on the deep brim of her bonnet.

As the sun beat down, filling her nostrils with the smell of hot leather, she gazed about, marvelling to see how the menace she had noticed on her journey with Captain Pensford had left the surrounding trees; today they merely looked lush and green, filled with the somnolent peace of a summer's day and peopled only by birds and butterflies.

Leahook was quiet and sleepy when they arrived, only a few small children playing in the dusty main street. Amy spared the Blue Anchor a glance as they swept by, half hoping that the landlady would look out and see her in such elegant company.

The horses stopped beside a row of small cottages and Lyddie explained as she and Jessie climbed down that they were making a visit to a sick woman who had once been employed at the Court.

'The driver will walk the horses round in a circle and pick them up when we return,' Medora told Amy, smiling a little maliciously as she noted the other girl's surprised glance. 'Of course, we could not expect you to be acquainted with such things.'

Amy stared at her thoughtfully, thinking how pretty she looked in her light muslin gown, with her hair glinting like gold beneath her fashionable bonnet.

Medora twirled the handle of her parasol, making lacy shadows pass over her face. 'Why are you looking at me like that?'

40

'I was thinking how pretty you are,' said the other truthfully, 'and what an unkind tongue you have!'

Sitting abruptly upright, Medora glared at her. 'How—how dare you talk to me like that!' she gasped. 'And I think, orphanage Miss, that if you wish to stay at the Court, you had best mind your own tongue.'

'I rather think the length of my stay depends upon Lady Kingsclear,' she said calmly.

Medora tossed her head. 'Grandmama will listen to me,' she said confidently. 'I believe I could make your visit both short and unpleasant—and I choose to.'

'It surprises me that so many of the inmates of Kingsclear Court should feel that my presence presents a challenge. You must all be very insecure...'

'I am Lady Kingsclear's granddaughter. What, pray are you?'

Sighing, Amy looked away, all her defiance melting under the painful question. 'I—don't know,' she owned.

'Precisely. A nobody, a foundling— probably a love child.'

Wincing at the scorn in the other's clear voice, Amy lifted her chin. 'I'd rather be that,' she said proudly, 'than a child of an arranged marriage, where husband and wife produce children as a loveless duty.'

'Lord!' sneered Medora, her eyes wide, 'how commonly vulgar!'

41

Amy's ready temper flared. 'How was London? I hear you had to leave before the end of the season,' she said pointedly.

Medora sucked in a breath as two bright spots of colour appeared in her cheeks. 'How did you know—if I thought Lyddie had told you—'

Amy realised how nearly she had betrayed her friend and made haste to cover her slip. 'No one told me anything,' she said quickly. 'From what Lady Kingsclear and others said, it wasn't hard to guess that you'd been sent down here to forget an unfortunate love affair.' She put out a hand in an appealing gesture. 'I'm sorry if I made you angry—can't we be friends?'

Glancing down at the proffered hand, Medora lifted her nose slightly in distain. 'I think not,' she said coldly, 'but while we are speaking so freely, Miss Clear, or whatever you call yourself, let me say that arranged marriages are "à la mode" in this family. If you think to make a good catch while you're at the Court, I'd advise you to look elsewhere. Neither Denvil or Ellis would consider you a fit object for—*matrimony*.'

Amy was amused. 'Surely you are not suggesting that either gentleman would seduce a guest of Lady Kingsclear's?' she asked and watched as the other flushed a little and dropped her eyes, making a pretence of fastening the strings of her parasol.

A rather frigid silence fell between them and Amy saw with some relief that they were approaching the row of cottages and that Lyddie and her companion were on the doorstep, taking their leave. Medora professed no interest in Amy's visit to the dressmaker and asked to be set down at the library.

'Have you and Medora quarrelled?' asked Lyddie anxiously, glancing back as the carriage headed away from the slim figure in the doorway.

'She seemed to think I needed warning that neither Mr Martin or Captain Pensford would marry me.'

Lyddie was puzzled. 'Why should she have supposed anything of the kind? Denvil is on the look out for an heiress, I know. His pockets are always to let, but as for Ellis, every time he has taken furlough from the Army, he has been the despair of husband-hunting Mama's with his indifference to any suitable girl produced.'

'I assure you,' smiled Amy, 'that until she put the thought into my head, I had not considered either gentleman in the role of prospective husband.'

'I have it,' exclaimed the other, the frown clearing from her forehead. 'Medora likes to hold court and usually when we are here and Denvil and Ellis are at home, they are only too willing to play at being her beau. Last night, at dinner, you must admit that they both showed an interest in you.'

'Certainly Mr Martin was very kind, but Captain Pensford showed more suspicion and watchfulness than anything else, I thought.'

'I believe he has never met anyone like you,' said Lyddie, simply. 'You are quite different to any of my friends or kinsfolk. You appear sure of yourself and self-possessed and yet—there is an air of vulnerability that presents a strange contrast.'

Amy blinked at her, surprised by her unexpected shrewdness. 'I had—hoped it didn't show,' she whispered, looking down at her hands in her lap.

Lyddie touched her hand. 'I find it appealing,' she smiled. 'So fierce and yet defenceless.' She looked round as they stopped outside a modest house, with a single hat displayed discreetly in a downstairs window and turned back to Amy. 'Let's choose your wardrobe and surprise them all.'

Mrs Mulchett was a lady of uncertain age, but of great presence and size, filling her small parlour to overflowing. Making no attempt at hiding her distain for Amy's attire, she brightened visibly at Lyddie's wish for a new wardrobe, thawing towards the other girl as she flung herself into the challenge with enthusiasm. As she and her staff had spent the winter months sewing muslin gowns that could be quickly altered to fit clients in immediate need, Amy's first wants were soon settled and the ladies turned their attentions to books of fashion plates and switches of material.

Amy was almost overcome by the huge choice presented before her and hesitated, at what seemed to her, to be wild extravagance. 'I cannot, surely, require three evening gowns?' she confided to the other girl.

'Indeed, I should think myself poorly done if I only had four at the beginning of the season,' said Lyddie. 'What a good thing that we are only in half mourning now and that you are only distantly related. I confess that I feel you need only be a little discreet and need not confine yourself to mauve or grey besides white.'

Amy removed her bonnet and the other's eyes fell admiringly on her nut-brown hair. 'Mrs Mulchett,' she called, 'Pray confirm what I say and persuade Miss Clear to have a green pelise.'

'Green, Madam, is your colour.' She obligingly held a mirror and draped a fold of green material under the girl's chin.

Amy gazed at herself in wonder; without the drab colours she habitually wore, her hair sprang to flame, framing a pale face, in which huge brown eyes glowed with excitement. Almost she could believe herself a beauty.

'Lilac would be in keeping,' went on Mrs Mulchett. 'And orange-tawney velvet for a riding-habit.'

'I don't ride—'

'I heard Grandmama asking Ellis to give you

45

lessons,' put in Lyddie, unaware of the consternation she aroused in her friend's breast.

At last, with her head reeling with the amount they had purchased, and filled with curious names and dazzled by colours, Amy was guided from the shop.

'Let me go back and cancel the half,' she pleaded on the doorstep. 'I cannot have need of so many things.'

Lyddie kept a firm hold on her arm, explaining that there was nothing chosen that a young lady with any pretention to fashion did not need.

'But—it must have cost a fortune—more than I earn in a year,' she protested weakly.

Lyddie shook her head, having a good idea of the bill that would be presented to her grandmother. 'Grandmama gave me a free hand,' she said, 'so don't worry.'

But Amy sat silent on the way home, filled with unease at having spent so much money on what could only be called the fripperies of life. Her frugal upbringing had not prepared her for such extravagance and the thought of so much wealth as, she was beginning to realise Lady Kingsclear possessed, was almost overwhelming. At last she understood why Captain Pensford had suspected her of being an adventuress.

The next day the muslin dresses arrived, complete with two velvet spencers, little high-waisted jackets in dark green and violet, with high necks and long sleeves. Lady Kingsclear having desired her presence, Amy presented herself to find that the maid, Jessie, was standing behind her mistress's chair.

'Did you enjoy your visit to the mantuamaker, child?' she was asked kindly.

'Very much, but—' she hesitated, uncertain how to proceed. 'I'm afraid it must have been very costly.'

The lady laughed. 'Have no fear. You'll not break my bankers,' she assured the girl. 'Well, Jessie?' she asked the silent woman behind her. 'What do you think?'

Amy found herself, once again, the object of a close scrutiny, but this time she was aware that the glance was friendly.

'I'd say, Ma'am, that you were right.'

The older woman exchanged meaning glances and Lady Kingsclear sighed audibly and closed her eyes momentarily. 'I thought so—but after all these years—hoping that some day ... I doubted my own judgement.'

'I'd know, Ma'am.'

'You most of all, Jessie.'

Gazing from one to the other, Amy was afraid to break into the strange conversation, yet knew that she was the subject of it. 'Lady Kingsclear—' she murmured tentatively, and at once her hands were taken and she was pulled to kneel at that lady's feet.

'My dear, I know what you are about to

47

ask—and can only beg of you to have a little patience. I promise you that I shall make all this mystery clear to you one day—in the meantime enjoy your stay here and accept me as your friend—your *loving* friend.'

A soft hand caressed her cheek, tears shone in Lady Kingsclear's faded eyes and Amy knew that, for the moment at least, she could ask no questions.

The older woman smoothed the shoulders of the girl's gown and re-tied the ribbon at her neck. 'I hope you chose a pretty wardrobe, child. I must admit that I find this gown vastly more becoming than that drab creation you were wearing yesterday.' She took Amy's chin and tilted her head. 'Let Jessie arrange your hair and I'll wager we'll have a beauty on our hands.'

The maid produced scissors and comb and curling tongs. Amy sat patiently under her hands as the skilled fingers snipped and arranged. At last it was done and a mirror was held before her. She stared in incredulity at the wide eyed, fashionable young lady that gazed back at her. Her hair was drawn into a smooth, gleaming coronet at the top of her head and soft curls framed her face.

'Oh, thank you, Jessie,' she breathed, turning her head to admire the effect.

'You'll do,' acknowledged the maid. 'Don't thank me, no one ever made a purse out of a sow's ear.'

'But you can gild the lily,' capped her mistress. 'Go and show yourself to Lyddie,' she suggested to Amy and both women watched indulgently as the girl ran from the room.

Lydia's admiration was genuine, but Medora, after shooting an angry glance at Amy, returned her attention to her desultory plucking at the notes of a pianoforte that stood in one corner of the room.

Soon a walk in the grounds was proposed and Amy and Lyddie went through the long windows that stood open onto the terrace and began to stroll over the smooth grass, where they were joined by Denvil Martin, who had seen them from the gun-room.

'Ladies,' he smiled and bowed, offering them both an arm, making no effort to hide his admiration as he looked at Amy. ''Pon my soul, when I left town, I had no idea of the delightful company I would find in the country. In future I shall look upon these retreats with more anticipation.'

Lydia laughed, obviously used to his flattery. 'Take no notice, Amy,' she advised. 'Denvil kissed the Blarney Stone in his youth and has been incorrigible ever since. Remember, Denvil, that we shall not always be here—we intend to stay the summer, but once Medora is again in favour, we shall return to Papa's keeping.'

'And Amy? What of her?'

Pale eyes were turned enquiringly in

49

her direction and she flushed a little uncomfortably under his gaze.

Seeing her discomfiture, he spoke quickly. 'Forgive me. I had not intended to pry, but as kin, I am interested in your movements.' He smiled down at her, his mouth curving gently, but an awareness at the back of his expression. 'And you *are* kin, are you not? I haven't the precise relationship ...?'

His words hung invitingly in the air and Amy was aware of the two faces turned to her for her answer.

'The exact relationship is a little difficult to unravel,' she said, with a show of indifference as she nipped off a flowerhead and held it to her nose to inhale the fragrance. 'Perhaps Lady Kingsclear could enlighten you.'

'No need,' said a voice crisply from behind them and they all swung round to confront the tall figure that had joined them unobserved. 'Even you, Denvil, must realise that with a name like Clear, she must be related to my uncle.'

A hard, grey gaze dared the other to ask more and, after a moment, Denvil Martin lowered his own eyes and hastily suggested a walk across the grounds to the ruins. Lyddie ran in to beg Medora to accompany them and soon they were heading towards the remains of the nunnery.

Medora seemed to have recovered from her sulks and was in high spirits, clinging to the

50

soldier's arm and talking animatedly as the breeze fluttered her narrow skirt and ruffled her blonde curls.

To Amy, Ellis Pensford seemed to attend to her with particular interest and attention and she could not but allow that she felt a slight envy of the two sisters and their handsome escorts.

Apparently recollecting her presence, Captain Pensford paused and half turning offered her his free arm. Slipping her hand into the crook of his elbow, Amy was aware of the darkling glance flung at her by Medora, but made pretence not to have seen it.

'How glad I am for your presence, Ellis,' said the other girl, 'for I vow I would never dare visit the ruins without a gentleman escort.'

'Pray enlighten me, Medora. Why ever not?'

Blue eyes sparkled soulfully up at him. 'Surely you remember our ghost?' she half whispered in throbbing tones. 'An I met a spectral Nun, I fear I should swoon away with fright.'

Ellis gave a short laugh. 'You should not have believed all those tales I told you in our childhood.'

'Well, I for one never believed the half,' put in Lyddie roundly. 'I remember your tales of black monks, phantom dogs and skeletons with clanking chains.'

'As a youth I must have had a fertile imagination,' commented the Captain dryly.

51

'You should follow my example and not believe all the tales you hear.'

Amy's glance flew to him and finding his gaze upon her, she looked hastily away, knowing the picture of guilt she must present. Chagrined, she pulled her hand away from his arm and he let her go without comment, seeming not to notice her withdrawal.

'But, you'll allow me a White Nun,' Medora was protesting. 'Why even Grandmama believes in her and only last winter one of the maids took a fit, having encountered a white shape on the stairs.'

'Bessie has been liable to such attacks since childhood,' put in Lydia's quiet tones and Medora pouted playfully at her sister.

Amy felt forgotten and wandered away by herself, anxious to explore the ruins, conscious of the conversation and laughter behind her. Sun-warmed stone gave back reflected heat, dazzling her eyes with its brightness and she was glad to find a shadowed cloister to walk along out of the sun's glare. To one side a low wooden door stood open and with mild curiousity Amy peered inside. Nothing more romantic met her eyes than brooms and scythes and other gardening implements piled neatly against the walls, while the corners were hidden in darkest gloom.

She was just turning away, when a movement behind gave warning a moment before hands pushed her violently and she stumbled forward into the chamber as the door closed with a dull thud behind her.

Blinded momentarily by the sudden transition to darkness, she felt her way to the door and beat her hands against it impotently. Something told her there was no use in pleading to be let out and she remained silent as she fumbled over the rough wood, feeling for a means of opening the door.

A few seconds later she knew that her prison could only be opened from outside and fought down her rising panic, trying to calm her fears, she looked about in the dim light that crept under the ill-fitting door, for a weapon. Rather than do nothing, she seized upon a thick billet of wood and began to beat on the solid door.

What seemed like hours later, she heard voices in the distance and thought she heard her name called. Redoubling her efforts, she shrieked wildly and was rewarded by the door suddenly being opened and sunlight flooding over her.

'My dear, Miss Clear,' said Ellis, taking the billet from her raised hand, 'there is no need for such energy.'

Giving a half sob, she turned away from the enquiring faces peering in at the door and tried to smooth her hair and disordered dress with hands that shook a little.

'What's to do?' the man said in quite a different voice and his touch was gentle as he took her shoulder and turned her to face him.

53

'Were you frightened?'

'They—used to do that at the orphanage,' Amy confessed, shaping her words with difficulty and fighting an almost overwhelming urge to fling herself on the broad shoulder so near.

Ellis Pensford interposed himself between the dishevelled girl and the interested cousins crowded in the doorway. 'Do you go on,' he said easily. 'Miss Clear and I will follow in a minute.'

Taking out a handkerchief, he tipped up her chin and removed the snail-like traces of tears and a smudge of dirt from her cheeks, before leaning his shoulders against the door post, he looked down at her and demanded an explanation.

'S-someone locked me in.'

One eyebrow raised inquiringly. 'Now, why should anyone do that?' he wondered.

'I don't know,' said Amy crossly, 'but they did.'

He pursed his lips thoughtfully. 'Much more likely to have been the wind,' he remarked calmly.

Amy looked past him to the still garden, not a branch or flowerhead moved. 'There is no wind.'

'But there was,' he pointed out. 'I distinctly remember seeing it move your curls.'

'That was Medora,' she answered without thought.

54

'To be sure,' he said and she could hear the amusement in his voice. 'How could I mistake blonde for red?' For a moment he smiled down at her, before proffering his arm. 'An you feel more composed we'll join the others.'

Somewhat reluctantly she laid her fingers on his sleeve and was discomfited when he covered them with his hand. 'I am sorry if you were frightened,' he said surprisingly.

She gave a little laugh that had a catch in it. 'I had forgotten—how much I disliked small cupboards ... and the dark.' Suddenly lifting her head, she confronted him. 'Who do you think shut me in there?' she asked bluntly.

'We had separated,' he told her. 'It could have been anyone. The gardener's boy, perhaps—or the wind. Take my advice, cousin and put it down to nature, or a somewhat thoughtless prank ... and don't dwell upon it too much.'

The others had been waiting in the Green Walk and as they joined them, Amy thought Medora's smile had a hint of triumph in it.

'What a good thing Ellis found you,' she thrilled, 'else you might have been there for ages.'

'That was hardly likely,' put in her sister, 'for we knew she could not be far away.'

'Medora would have it that the White Nun had you in her ghostly clutches,' smiled Denvil, 'but I was more inclined to the fairies having claimed one of their own.'

55

Amy smiled dutifully at his whimsy, but suddenly the enjoyment had gone from the day, looking round at their faces, she couldn't help but wonder which one had closed the door on her and shivered involuntarily at the thought that someone at Kingsclear Court should dislike her enough to want to frighten her.

CHAPTER FOUR

Soon Amy's wardrobe began arriving from Mrs Mulchett's busy establishment and when the new orange-tawney riding-habit was unpacked she knew that she no longer had an excuse to put off the dreaded riding lessons.

'How delightful!' exclaimed Lyddie, holding the bright velvet folds against herself. 'I vow it makes me envious. And such a dashing hat— just like the shakos the soldiers wear. You'll make Ellis feel quite at home when he sees you.'

But when the next day arrived, Amy reluctantly crept down to the stables to meet him, she read only cool appraisal in his grey eyes as he turned from a groom and studied her as she stood hesitantly in the doorway.

'Good morning, cousin,' he greeted her. 'Come into the yard and we'll arrange a mount for you.' His fingers nipped her elbow as he led her back across the cobbled yard.

Unable to hide her start of alarm at the sight of a huge, black horse that was being led towards them, she glanced quickly up into her companion's face and was disconcerted to find a smile at the back of his eyes.

'Pray don't alarm yourself,' he said coolly. 'That is my animal.' Pulling down the proud, black head, he searched in his pocket and proffered a piece of sugar. 'Make friends with him,' he suggested, seeming unaware of her reluctance. 'Duke—be nice to the lady.'

'D-Duke?' she questioned standing still and wishing heartily that she was back in the secure orphanage where she had never been called upon to make friends with anything bigger than a small child.

Brown fingers caressed the long Roman nose of the horse. 'After the Duke himself,' Captain Pensford told her. 'Don't you know the troops call him "Old Beaky"? Not to his face, of course.'

Amy looked down at the sugar, sparkling in the palm of her hand and bit her lip unhappily, while the animal clattered his hooves impatiently and seemed to tower over her, as he blew softly through his nostrils.

'Give him the sugar, Miss Clear,' said his master and Amy realised that Ellis Pensford was quite aware of her fears. 'The sugar,' he repeated inexorably, and she met his eyes, lifting her chin a little as she took a breath and stepped forward, her palm out-stretched.

Soft lips nuzzled her hand and warm breath moistened her fingers. In a minute the ordeal was over and she was surprised at how easily it had been accomplished. Before she could step back her hand was imprisoned and carried to the horse's velvet nose.

'Pet him, Miss Clear and finish a good job,' said Ellis and, inspite of her quick attempt to withdraw, he smoothed her hand over the animal's warm flesh.

Standing so close behind her that she could almost feel his presence, Amy was very aware of the soldier's great height and breadth of shoulder, wondering uncomfortably if he knew the unsettling effect his nearness was having upon her.

'Well done,' he said surprisingly. 'You're over the first hurdle, cousin.'

Looking up quickly at the unexpected praise, Amy was in time to see him turn away as a groom brought a small, grey mare across the cobbles to them.

'This is more your weight,' Ellis said, taking the bridle. 'She belongs to my sister and there isn't an ounce of vice in her—Lyddie tells me that it's more like sitting in an arm chair than riding a horse.'

He smiled down at her, encouragingly and Amy swallowed convulsively, knowing that the moment she had been dreading had arrived. Giving the bridle back to the waiting groom, Captain Pensford led her to the mounting block and explained how to sit in the side-saddle.

'If you were younger I'd teach you to ride astride first,' he said, 'but Aunt Charlotte would not have us flout the conventions, so you'll have to learn to ride in that ridiculous position. Remember to keep your knee round the pommel flexed and the other tight in the stirrup.'

Swinging himself up into his own saddle, he took the leading rein from the groom and the horses walked sedately into the paddock backing onto the stable-yard.

Amy held her breath and closed her eyes as she clutched wildly at the saddle for support.

'Sit up,' she was told. 'Hold the reins loosely—and *look where you're going*!'

The tone the soldier used brooked no argument and the girl's eyes flew open to see the earth far beneath her, jogging by in the most alarming manner. Her fingers tightened in panic and she took a quick, frightened breath.

'I'm here beside you—you're quite safe,' said a voice comfortingly and somewhat to her surprise, Amy felt a slight lessening of her fears.

Under his patient tuition she began to relax, finding the animal she rode surprisingly docile and kind. She had just discovered that she might enjoy this new experience, when Captain

Pensford decided that the lesson had lasted long enough and turned the horses' heads towards the stables.

'Well, cousin?' he asked, leaning out of the saddle to open the barred gate with the tip of his riding-crop. 'Will you admit that your fears were groundless?'

His light coloured eyes under the curly brim of his tall hat held a slight smile and Amy allowed herself to smile a little in return, rather enjoying the unusual feeling of accord between them.

'I'll own to a little nervousness—'

'I had suspected as much,' the man acknowledged gravely.

She darted him a swift, suspicious glance, but went on, 'I must confess that I found you a more patient teacher than I had imagined.'

Ellis lifted his head in a laugh. 'Good God, Miss Clear, were you more afraid of me than the horse?'

Amy considered, her head on one side under the dashing military shako. 'I believe you were about equal,' she admitted demurely as the groom came forward to take the leading rein and Captain Pensford slid easily to the ground despite the handicap of having one arm in a sling.

Looking down at him uncertainly, she wondered how to dismount, encumbered as she was among the heavy folds of her long skirt. Reading her hesitation Ellis came to her side.

'Unhook your leg, put your hands on my shoulders and I'll gainsay to bring you safe to terra-firma,' he told her.

Amy glanced down into his dancing eyes and felt her heart lurch unexpectedly. 'Y-Your arm?' she queried.

'Will take your feather weight,' he affirmed, tugging it free of the black silken folds across his chest. 'I wear it more for comfort and support now. Soon I shall leave it off altogether.'

He held his arms up invitingly and she launched herself trustingly towards the earth. His hands closed round her waist and, for a moment she was held suspended before being deposited, flushed and laughing on the cobbles of the yard.

Ellis looked down at her and at something in his expression she grew sober and gazed thoughtfully back at him, her eyes suddenly troubled under the modish peak of her cap. Slowly he looked her over, from the military style hat and smart soldier-like frogging on the short jacket of her riding-habit, to the long fold of her skirt clutched in one hand, showing a pair of small elegant boots. His eyes had grown cool by the time they found her face again.

'You seem a different creature to the one I found waiting me at Leahook,' he stated flatly.

Amy shivered, suddenly chilled and with an effort looked away, until only the curve of her

61

cheek could be seen under the peak of her hat. 'Sometimes I feel a different person,' she admitted in a small voice. 'The orphanage seems another life—something I have no wish to remember.'

'Perhaps you had best make an effort to improve your memory,' he said, taking her arm and leading her towards the house. 'Has Lady Kingsclear set any date for your stay?'

Dumbly she shook her head. Suddenly the enjoyment had gone from the day, leaving her unsecure and uncertain.

His voice spoke from above her head. 'Take my advice, Miss Clear and remember your origins, whatever they may be—I think you would be wise not to bank on too long a stay here.'

'I would remind you, sir, that your aunt seems to know more about my origins than I do,' she said quickly, trying to hide her anger. 'As for my visit here, I believe that is my own affair and Lady Kingsclear's, who is my hostess.'

She tried to break free, but his grip tightened on her elbow, holding her prisoner. 'True,' her captor agreed, stopping on the gravel drive and turning her to face him. 'I did but remind you that your visit here could end as abruptly as it began. My aunt is a woman of moods and whims. Her wish to have you here could change as quickly as her sudden interest was aroused ... and I would have you prepared for such an eventuality.'

Amy looked up at him, her eyes sparkling and high spots of temper in her cheeks. 'Then—I could return to being a governess,' she said as evenly as her quickened breathing would allow. 'Doubtless Lady Kingsclear would be so kind as to give me a character recommendation.'

Shaking his hand from her arm, she found herself free as he stood back, and, tossing the long orange folds of her skirt over her arm, she broke away and ran into the house, leaving the man looking after her thoughtfully.

'How did you get on?' called Lyddie, hanging over the banisters as she came into the hall.

Amy pulled off her modish hat and ran her fingers through her hair as she began to climb the stairs to join her friend. 'Quite well, I suppose,' she answered dispiritedly.

'Was Ellis a hard taskmaster?' asked the other sympathetically.

'Not particularly. In fact it was all much better than I had thought it would be.'

'Why are you in the dismals, then?'

'He reminded me that all this cannot go on for ever, that sometime my visit here must come to an end. I suppose he looked at my habit and remembered how I was dressed when I first came here ... and thought I was taking advantage of Lady Kingsclear's kindness.'

Lyddie looked thoughtful. 'I don't see why it

63

can't go on—I think it very likely that my Grandmama will offer you a position, perhaps as her companion for I believe that she has taken a fondness to you. Medora was remarking upon it the other day.'

'Do you really?' Amy sighed and looked at the panelled passages leading off from the landing and the carved stairs she had just climbed. 'I must admit I should miss all this, an I had to leave.'

'Well, if Grandmama turns you off without a penny, I shall persuade Papa to engage you as my companion—but I have discovered something of great interest,' she suddenly said mysteriously and, sliding her arm through her friend's she began to draw her along the passage towards Lady Kingsclear's rooms.

'I remember being told as a child that this portrait had been removed from the hall downstairs because of some disgrace or other and this morning when I was on my way to see Grandmama I happened to notice the likeness.' She stood back triumphantly, allowing Amy a clear view of the painting hanging above their heads and waited for her reaction.

The other girl stared up at the portrait in its huge gilt frame. As she took in the dark eyes and nut-brown hair, her lips fell open in surprise. Involuntarily her hand crept to her mouth as with a half stifled exclamation, she turned to the other girl.

'W-Who is it?'

'I don't know, the name plate has been removed, but he's the image of you, isn't he?'

Amy looked back at the painting, noticing the shape of the face, which could have been her own and the slightly old fashioned clothes the sitter wore. 'We—must find out who he is,' she said slowly.

'Here's Jessie,' Lydia whispered. 'We'll ask her—she's sure to know,' and raised her voice as the elderly maid approached, with a tray for her mistress's mid-morning refreshment.

'Why, that's Master Aubrey, your Grandmother's only son,' she was told shortly. 'Him as I was nursemaid to.'

She made to go on, but Lyddie put a hand on her arm to detain her. 'Tell us about him,' she pleaded.

The older woman's eyes flickered from one young face to the other and then upwards to the painted eyes that seemed to meet her own. Almost reluctantly she looked at Amy and a sigh escaped her.

'Please,' Amy added her pleas to her friend's and Jessie's eyes softened.

Balancing the laden tray on her hip, she gazed up at the young man and smiled slightly. 'I had charge of Master Aubrey from the moment he was born,' she said reminiscently, 'and a lovely babe he was—and grew up into a sweet child. Everyone loved him, for all he was an imp of mischief and always into trouble.'

65

'Yes, but what happened to him?' asked Lyddie impatiently, as the older woman fell silent and seemed lost in her thoughts.

'He died young ... years ago,' she was told curtly and the maid hitched up her tray and would say nothing more as she continued on her way to Lady Kingsclear.

'I'm sure there's a mystery,' whispered Lyddie, staring after her retreating back. 'Do you think he could be your father?'

Amy's dark eyes opened wide. 'Oh, Lyddie,' she breathed, 'that would make us cousins. I'd have a family of my own.'

For a while that possibility was enough; filling her mind to the exclusion of all other thoughts, but gradually she came to wonder at the reason for Lady Kingsclear's reticence to talk about her relationship and began to wonder about the mystery of her own birth.

Each day Captain Pensford gave her a riding lesson and, while she would never be as talented a rider as Medora, quite soon she was competent in the saddle and a day's excursion to a beauty spot several miles distant was arranged.

As it was a family party, the girls were to be allowed to go without the presence of an older woman or a duenna and the thought of such freedom filled Lydia and her sister with delight.

'In London we would have had to bear the company of our old governess,' confided Lyddie to Amy. 'She is the nicest creature

66

imaginable, but her presence does rather detract from the enjoyment of such an outing.'

Amy, who had only ever had the company of a small maid from the orphanage on her infrequent outings or shopping expeditions, smiled sympathetically and privately hoped she would acquit herself well the next day.

That evening the sky was eagerly watched for the signs of red that would signify good weather for the morrow and the elderly gardener, well known as a weather prophet, earnestly quizzed as to his opinion. Clear, pale skies were met the next morning with universal relief and the girls met in their riding habits to partake of an early breakfast.

Soon Denvil Martin came to tell them that the horses were ready and, accompanied by a young groom on a sturdy cob, carrying two wicker baskets containing their luncheon, they set out along the winding drive to the gates of the park.

Looking back at the Court Amy caught sight of Lady Kingsclear in her window and raised one arm to wave to her, before they turned the corner by the lake and the house was lost to view.

Ellis was waiting for them by the entrance to his estate and as he came towards them on his big black horse, Amy glanced over his shoulder, eager to catch sight of the house behind him. Raven Hall had been built before the reign of Queen Elizabeth and much added to since. Grey timbers and yellow brick work under a stone roof gave the impression of having mellowed together with the surrounding walled gardens and terraces. Flowers and shrubs rioted over the flowerbeds, presenting a very different appearance to the formal array of Kingsclear Court.

'You appear to approve of my house?'

Amy started and averted her eyes, aware that she had been staring blatantly. 'I—had imagined it quite different,' she told him.

'Indeed?' Black eyebrows flew up into twin peaks as he quizzed her. 'Pray enlighten me.'

'I thought Raven Hall would be modern, white perhaps, with colonnades and built in the Palladian style. I had not suspected that you cared for our own English antiquities.'

'Perhaps, Miss Clear, you don't know me very well.' His saddle creaked as he swung his mount in beside her. 'Maybe we can become better acquainted today.' Glancing down at her as they rode together, his eyebrows drew a little together. 'Now what,' he wondered, 'can I have said to banish the smile from your face?'

The girl threw him a challenging glance. 'I had thought that the outing was intended to be a holiday,' she remarked. 'You have quite cast me down with the thought of a catechism awaiting me.'

'I have no intention of spoiling your day,' he answered soberly, 'but hoped rather that we could come to know each other better in these

68

different circumstances.'

Amy wondered a little at his unexpected offer of friendship, but was saved from replying by the fact that the others had waited in the lane ahead and that now they joined them and conversation became general for a while.

'May I say, cousin Amy, that you have done remarkably well in your riding lessons?' said Denvil, falling in beside her.

'I had a good teacher.'

'And I an apt pupil,' called Captain Pensford over his shoulder. 'An you had begun riding in your childhood, you would have made an excellent horsewoman.'

'As usual, Ellis you are generous with your praise,' said Medora sweetly. 'I'm sure that Amy knows, as well as any of us, that her apparent ability is due to your tuition.'

Amy flushed a little at this exchange and the little grey mare, sensing her feelings, danced eagerly, sending up puffs of white dust from her small neat hooves. Aware that her companions were watching, Amy controlled her, tightening the knee that was round the saddle pommel until her mount grew calm and consented to walk forward.

'Well done,' murmured Denvil Martin for her ears alone and, turning her head, she read admiration in his eyes and smiled with pleasure. 'You make a delightful picture,' he told her. 'Your habit almost matches your hair

69

'... who'd have supposed that you would have the Kingsclear colouring so plainly?'

Looking away, she was conscious of his eyes upon her, examining the curve of her cheek under the light brown curls, taking in the shape of her nose and following the thin lines of her arched eyebrows.

'I have the distinct feeling that you remind me of someone...' he said slowly, almost to himself and then went on in a louder tone. 'I wager that you have put Medora's nose out of joint.'

She looked up quickly. 'How so?'

'She is used to being the beauty of the family. An I am not mistaken she'll not take kindly to being eclipsed.'

Amy looked ahead to the vivacious figure in cornflower blue, her blonde curls dancing under an elegant little top hat set at a becoming angle. 'She is very beautiful—I would like to think that I was as pretty,' she said frankly.

'You are not in the same style, but there are others who would think you the more attractive,' Denvil told her, his eyes bold in his too obvious admiration. 'You do well to rival her.'

Made a little uneasy by his attempts at a flirtation, Amy smiled a trifle coolly and urged her horse forward to join Lyddie, who turned to smile at her.

'I believe we are nearly there,' she said. 'Are you weary?'

70

Amy shook her head. 'Not a bit,' she said gaily. 'To my surprise I find I like riding.'

'You have overcome your fear of horses very well.'

Medora flung an impatient glance over her shoulder, but only expressed a wish that they had gone somewhere else, for she was finding such an easy ride rather insipid.

'Then let us take a gallop across this open plain,' suggested the soldier, as the road they were travelling came to an end and a vista of rolling downs and open countryside confronted them.

With a whoop Medora set her mount into a gallop, closely followed by the black stallion and after a moment Denvil set off after them, leaving Lyddie and Amy to follow more sedately.

'Do go after them an you wish,' said Amy, but the other girl shook her head, saying she preferred to look about and talk.

When they came up with the others, they found that the place for the picnic luncheon had been selected, high on the side of the rounded hill, sheltered by low thorn bushes from the prevailing wind. Leaving the horses in the care of the young groom, the girls set out the meal, while the two men climbed to a vantage point to scan the surrounding views with the aid of a small spyglass Ellis had had the forethought to bring.

Amy felt her eyes widen as the food baskets

were unpacked, but found that the fresh air had sharpened her appetite and that she was able to do justice to the 'al fresco' meal.

Afterwards they explored their surroundings in rather a desultory manner. Medora called her sister and Amy found herself alone. Sitting down, she leaned her chin in her hand, gazing at the hazy view that stretched away at the foot of the hill. The nearby voices grew dim as the sun warmed her back and her eyelids began to droop drowsily. Almost asleep, she was aware that someone had stretched themself beside her and turned her head quickly.

'Tired, Miss Clear?' asked Captain Pensford, crossing his long legs in their tight riding breeches and setting the tiny gold tassels swinging on his shiny black boots.

'Not really—I find this rather overwhelming. The country is new to me. Until I left Portsmouth I had never seen so much open space ... unless you count the sea, of course, but that had the Isle of Wight not far away.'

'I know. I've embarked from Portsmouth harbour many times.' He smiled lazily up at her. 'Perhaps we've passed in the street.'

'Oh, no!' she said involuntarily. 'I should have remembered—' and broke off in confusion, colouring under his quizzical gaze.

Plucking a blade of grass, he chewed the end thoughtfully. 'My gardener tells me that the strawberries, that are the pride of his life, will soon be ripe—you must all come over to the Hall one afternoon and we'll arrange a tea party. I'll show you around the house at the same time. It's very remiss of me to have left it so long without inviting you.'

Amy glanced down at her hands in her lap, veiling her eyes with her dark lashes. 'I am well aware that I do not stand in the usual role of guest,' she said in a low tone. 'I can understand that my presence must present difficulties of etiquette...'

'I assure you that, if we are to be cousins in the eyes of the world, nothing must stand between our easy communion,' he told her blandly. 'My sister, whom I had hoped would play the part of my hostess this summer has taken herself off to help nurse a batch of children through an outbreak of measles. I cannot imagine why she should have thought cousin Bella's needs greater than mine, but it is so and I find that I can only invite ladies to my house for the most innocuous of entertainments without inviting censure from the local matrons.'

Amy bit her lips at the plaintive note in his voice. 'I had not suspected that you cared so much for others' opinion,' she said in shaking tones. 'Confess, sir, that you much prefer to have your house to yourself and not be called upon to act host to dinner parties and routs.'

Ellis Pensford tilted his hat the better to

shade his eyes and allowed a smile to curve his mouth. 'Cousin Amy,' he murmured, 'surely you can't suppose that I would prefer my own company to that of my three lovely kinswomen?'

Unused to the company of men and such easy intimacies as he and his cousin seemed to expect from her, she felt his flirtatious manner was in danger of going to her head and deliberately drew back a little.

'I believe one could almost see to Portsmouth from here,' she remarked brightly.

'Not in this direction,' she was told dryly as Captain Pensford dropped his spyglass into her lap. 'Amuse yourself with that, child,' he suggested and apparently tired of her conversation, closed his eyes and seemed prepared for sleep.

Amy hesitated uncertainly, before scrambling to her feet, she made her way to a nearby vantage point and trained the glass on a distant church spire. At once the stonework sprang into detail and she was unable to stifle an exclamation of amazement. Entranced by her new toy, she spent many happy minutes examining the locality and was surprised, when Lyddie called her, to see that the hour was far advanced into the afternoon and that the others were preparing to set off on the homeward journey.

Shyly she gave back his belonging to Ellis, suddenly aware as he slipped it into an inner pocket that he had discarded the black sling he had worn since she knew him.

'I am glad that your arm is better,' she said.

'I find that I can rest it inside my coat if need be without the sling proclaiming my disability to all the world.'

Medora had come up and, standing nearby, was obviously listening. 'Ellis,' she put in, 'such a wound is a distinction not to be hidden away. I assure you that we are proud of our soldier kinsman, bearing his scars of battle. You must know that your black sling made all our female hearts more susceptible. I for one found it most attractive—'

'Medora,' he said, taking her hand and gallantly kissing the tips of her fingers, 'had I known that the French had presented me with such a weapon to set your heart aflutter, I would have taken care to wear it for the rest of my life. But what am I to do? ... an I put it back, you'll all know me for a fraud!'

'Doubtless a few sighs and knitted brows will serve to remind us,' Lyddie said dryly, as she allowed Denvil to toss her up into her saddle. 'Perhaps it will be like Grandpapa's gout and you'll be able to forecast the weather by it.'

'Lyddie, you lack a romantic soul,' her cousin told her and helped Medora to mount before turning to perform the same service for Amy.

The memory of the journey back to

Kingsclear Court in the mellow warmth of the drowsy early evening, would always remain with Amy; the call of the blackbirds in the hedges, the scent that arose from the hedge flowers as the horses brushed against them, filled her with content and, when at last, the gates of the Court came into view, she lifted her head and stared at the undulating parkland and magnificent trees with a feeling of homecoming, wishing only that that particular moment of happiness could last for ever.

CHAPTER FIVE

During her stay at Kingsclear Court Amy had discovered that although Lady Kingsclear often stayed in her room and was generally cossetted, whenever she liked that lady would dress herself elegantly and depart on a visit to a friend or attend a dinner party that promised to be particularly enjoyable.

'Grandmama has found that a little— weakness can be rewarding,' Lyddie told her, her eyes twinkling. 'Before Grandpapa died he lived a very active life and she was always being called upon to do something or undertake some new duty and a mild invalidism was her one retreat. Sir William was a vigorous, energetic man and to some extent she had to be the same, but now she has discovered how pleasant it is to be deferred to and waited upon.'

Amy thought back to the plump figure of Lady Kingsclear reclining against cushions while conversing languidly and found difficulty in imagining her even being mildly active however much her husband desired it, but she found that the lady in question could be surprisingly energetic when the mood took her.

One morning when entering Lady Kingsclear's room for their usual visit, the girls found her already up and sitting at her dressing-table while Jessie arranged her hair.

'Go and pretty yourselves my loves,' she cried, seeing their surprised faces in the mirror. 'It's time we took Amy to meet our friends. I intend to pay several morning calls and leave cards to show I am in half mourning now and can accept invitations once more. You girls have rusticated enough—'tis time we were more lively.'

Initiated into the mysteries of morning calls by Lydia, Amy was surprised to discover how many ten minute visits could be crammed into one morning and amazed at the numbers of cards that could be left at various doors by the footman while the ladies sat in their carriage.

'*Now* we shall begin to enjoy ourselves,' Medora murmured with satisfaction. 'I vow I was ready to die with boredom!'

Amy noticed, however, that she was careful that her grandmother did not hear and that the face she turned to her was attentive and smiling, even if a frown appeared whenever Amy was introduced as a kinswoman.

Within days the visits were returned and soon invitations began to appear in the mantelshelf, however the first event was to be an informal country dance given by Lady Kingsclear for the young people of the district.

Amy found herself looking forward to it with mixed feelings, knowing that she would be on view to the local gentry and that her entry into society depended upon her own success and the favour with which the various Mama's viewed her.

As it was her first dance Lady Kingsclear insisted upon her wearing white and chose a virginal creation for her. Even though she had longed for yellow crepe, when the dress of satin with an over gown of spangled gauze arrived Amy gasped and knew herself quite won over.

'You look like Queen Mab,' approved Lyddie eyeing her friend on the night of the dance. 'Mrs Mulchett has surpassed herself.'

Smoothing the folds of her dress with gentle fingers, Amy's eyes sparkled with happiness and excitement as they walked down the corridor to show themselves to Lady Kingsclear, but most of her effervescent mood evaporated at sight of Medora. The blonde girl was wearing a cream satin gown with a half train so devastating in its cut and simplicity that Amy felt at once that her own ensemble was country made and over ornate. Medora smiled at her across the room and the other girl knew that the effect had been calculated and designed to spoil her pleasure.

'My dear, you look delightful,' cooed Lady Kingsclear. 'So fresh and—virginal!'

'Almost like a school miss,' put in Medora maliciously.

'An air of over-worldly languor doesn't become us all,' remarked her sister, taking Amy's hand in a comforting grasp as Medora turned away with a flounce.

'You need a necklace, my dear,' remarked Lady Kingsclear suddenly.

Amy put a hand to her throat. 'I'm afraid I don't own anything suitable,' she confessed and felt the embarrassed colour rise to her cheeks.

'Jessie, bring me my jewel box,' commanded the elder woman. 'I think I have just the thing for you ... here it is and just right for that dress.' She brought out a small string of pearls and, gesturing to Amy to kneel down, clasped them round her neck.

'Grandmama—your pearls!' protested Medora. 'I wore them to my first ball.'

'And so did Lyddie,' her grandmother pointed out calmly.

The implication of her act struck Amy and Medora at the same time and for a second their eyes met and clashed until the other girl swung away, her face flushed with anger and Amy

79

turned back to the seated woman, her own eyes wide with an unspoken question.

Lady Kingsclear's own expression held a strange longing as she touched the girl's cheek in a brief caress. 'Run along,' she said softly, 'the first guests will be arriving soon and I must be ready to meet them. Wait for me at the foot of the stairs.'

When she joined them, resplendent in black crepe and jet ornaments, the first guests could be heard arriving and Lady Kingsclear took her place beside the girls as the coach drew up outside. Amy was introduced to so many people that her head spun, luckily she was required to do no more than give them her hand and curtsey, but even so she was well aware that she was the object of much speculation and the subject of many whispered conversations.

The occupants of the Court had dined in their bedchambers so that the huge dining-room might be cleared for dancing and a cold supper laid in the breakfast room, while a few discreet card tables were set up in the green parlour for the guests who did not care to take the floor.

Amy was aware that Captain Pensford had arrived, having found herself at the end of his quick scrutiny, but was somewhat relieved when she discovered that Denvil Martin was to lead her out for the first dance.

'Run along, child,' smiled Lady Kingsclear

as he approached. 'Enjoy yourself—but remember more than two dances with any gentleman would give rise to comment.' Giving her a parting nod that set her black feathers aquiver as Denvil crooked his elbow invitingly, the elder lady set off in search of her own cronies.

The Cotillion was accomplished easily and Amy was grateful for the hours spent practising with Lyddie. After that the requests came quickly and she found her card almost full when Ellis Pensford strolled lazily up to her and bowed.

Looking at his gleaming head, Amy had to admit that evening dress became him almost as well as the bright red regimentals. Diamonds sparkled from the snowy folds of his cravat, his dark blue coat fitted his broad shoulders without a wrinkle and his legs were long and elegant in the unaccustomed black evening breeches and silk stockings he wore.

Meeting her regard as he straightened, his grey eyes quizzed her slightly. 'I hope I meet with your approval,' he said, a teasing note in his voice.

Amy dimpled a little, but answered frankly. 'I've not seen you in formal dress before—and I see that you have discarded your sling.'

'I could hardly dance handicapped in that way,' he pointed out. 'I came, Miss Clear, to petition a dance from you—an you still have a space for me to write my name.'

Amy glanced down at her card. 'I am free for the round dance after supper,' she told him and, taking the card out of her hand, he put his initials upon it, before leaving her to the care of a young gentleman who had presented himself to claim her as his partner for the dance that was just forming.

To her surprise, Amy found that she was looking forward to the dance with the soldier and even the darkling glances from Medora's bright eyes as she spoke to Captain Pensford left her quite unprepared for the attack launched upon her. The icy glint of his grey eyes as he bent over her hand should have warned her of impending danger, but she stepped forward unwarily, allowing herself to be guided into place as the music began.

'I see you are wearing the Kingsclear pearls,' he remarked suddenly as the couples faced each other.

Concentrating on the movements of the dance Amy did not reply for a moment. 'Yes— was it not kind of her?'

'Kind indeed!'

Something in his tone made her glance up quickly to receive the full force of his angry stare like a douche of cold water in her face. Missing her step, she faltered and was ruthlessly drawn back into place by his grip on her wrist. Raising her bewildered face to his, she would have spoken but his voice cut across hers before she could ask a question.

'Don't play the Green Miss with me, girl. Medora has told me how you inveigled that string of pearls from Lady Kingsclear.'

'Inveigled! Indeed, I did no such thing,' Amy protested indignantly.

Thin black eyebrows rose to questioning peaks. 'Medora is not telling the truth when she says you told her grandmother that you possessed no jewels?'

Amy dropped her gaze. 'I did say that,' she confessed miserably, 'but truly I had no intention—'

The dance took them apart and for a while they were forced to smile and bow to another couple, before the movement brought them together again and the girl could go on with her explanation.

'I had no idea of Lady Kingsclear's intentions.'

'And made no demur when she offered you the pearls, I wager.'

'No—why should I?' She made no attempt to hide her puzzlement.

'Even when you must have realised their worth and when Medora told you that she and Lydia had worn them to their first ball? You must have understood the implications in the act.'

Eyes widening, she gazed up at him, her mouth opened a little with her quickened breathing. 'You—think I set out deliberately to make Lady Kingsclear acknowledge me!'

she gasped and suddenly all the kindness and attention she had received that evening from the local gentry invited to the Court turned to bitter gall. Glancing round, every eye seemed to be turned on her in speculation and, abruptly, her one desire was to leave the brightly lit room and watching people.

Turning on her heel, she half broke away, but before she could leave the set, fingers closed round her wrist and she was held in her place.

'Dance, Miss Clear,' said an inexorable voice in her ear. 'You are mistaken if you think to make me the object of gossip or speculation. We'll finish this dance together as though we are the best of friends and then you will act in a perfectly normal way for the rest of the evening. If you think I will allow you to make the Kingsclears the object of local scandal, you are quite wrong.'

Glancing up at him, Amy could only see through a blur of tears and blinked furiously, determined that none should fall. Instinct set her feet in the right steps, but even so the dance seemed interminable as Ellis Pensford's cool hands held her, his presence making her a prisoner. At last the music ended and she turned from him in undisguised relief, but at once his hand took her elbow before she could escape and she was guided back to her seat and the watchful eyes of her hostess.

'You look tired, child,' she said kindly, noticing the girl's pale face. 'Sit by me for a while. Luckily these informal affairs are not expected to go on too long and you'll see the guests will start leaving soon.'

Amy forced a weary smile and allowed the older woman to make excuses when her partner came to claim her. Leaning back, she felt the beginnings of a headache at the back of her eyes, but found that Lady Kingsclear had been right and that couples came to thank their hostess and to bid her goodnight.

At last only the family remained in the hall and Amy's heart began to thump uncomfortably against her high waisted bodice as Captain Pensford left Lyddie and Medora and came towards her.

'Aunt Charlie,' he said, taking that lady's hand and conveying it to his lips. 'As usual your entertainment was as superb as yourself.'

Lady Kingsclear smiled fondly at him. 'I'm too old for your flattery, Ellis,' she told him. 'Save such pretty remarks for your cousins and Amy.'

Grey eyes flickered briefly in her direction and Amy flinched a little. 'I find that Miss Clear has no liking for my conversation,' he remarked curtly and turned away to make his farewells to his cousins.

'Ellis on his high horse?' asked Lady Kingsclear with interest.

Amy hung her head. 'I am afraid that he suspects me of being an adventuress,' she confessed unhappily.

85

The plumes of Lady Kingsclear's headdress quivered. 'Indeed? I had not suspected my nephew of possessing so vivid an imagination.' She patted Amy's cheek. 'Away to bed, child— bring me the pearls and I'll lock them away safe in my jewel-case.'

Amy followed her ample form up the stairs, aware of Ellis's gaze on her as she climbed. At the landing, she turned almost involuntarily, looking down at the darkening hall as the servants began their task of snuffing the dying candles and found that the soldier had followed her to the first step of the stairs and was staring after her.

For a moment their eyes met, his gaze enigmatic in the flickering light, before he turned abruptly away, calling for his caped overcoat and tall hat.

Not waiting to see him leave, the girl swung on her heel and ran to her room. The candles that had been lit several hours earlier had burnt low in their sockets. Going to the dressing-table she stared into the mirror, the dancing shadows and dim glow giving her an ethereal appearance, making her dark eyes huge and cavernous in her pale face.

For a few seconds she gazed back at her reflection, her bosom rising and falling agitatedly, before she lifted her hands and unclasped the pearls from about her neck. Heavy and smooth, they lay like a snake coiled in the palm of her hand. She regarded them almost with revulsion, then closed her fingers over them and went quickly along the corridor to Lady Kingsclear's room.

'There's a good girl,' said the older woman approvingly, seeing her errand. 'Put them in my jewel-box and I'll lock it in a minute. I'm waiting for Medora's bracelet, but if I know that young lady, she'll go to bed with never a thought for its safety and bring it to me in the morning with a pretty excuse.'

But there was to be no excuse on Medora's lips, pretty or otherwise. Amy was just putting the finishing touches to her toilet the next morning, when a commotion in the corridor made her pause and turn her head to listen as the sound of an angry altercation came to her ears. After a moment she went to her door and opened it in time to see Lydia dash past obviously following her sister who was hurrying towards her grandmother's chamber. The other girl sent her an eloquent glance as she went by and sometime later, returned as Amy had known she would.

'Such a fuss and bother!' she exclaimed as she entered precipitously and closed the door smartly behind her. 'Such a commotion as you never did hear.'

'I heard only too well,' commented Amy dryly. 'What is it?'

'Medora has lost a bracelet—one she sets much store by as Grandpapa gave it to her when she came out. And now she will have it

87

that someone has stolen it—as though a robber broke in last night while we slept and, disdaining all other valuables, took only that!'

'Was it very valuable?'

'I believe so, Grandmama always locks it away in her jewel-box.'

'Oh, yes ... she did say something last night about waiting for it.'

'Well, she's as mad as fire with Medora for not bringing it to her and is setting the servants on to search the house.'

'She doesn't believe in the selective burglar, then?'

'More like the careless miss, I'd say,' said Lyddie knowledgeably and looked around restlessly. 'Have you ever noticed how flat everything is after some social activity. 'Tis always so, after a ball or dinner, I've noticed often.'

Amy smiled. 'You must know that last night was the first dance I've ever attended and I can only confess to a little tiredness.' Even as she spoke, she knew that she had told only half the truth. In reality the morning was dull and she felt lethargic and depressed, but not even to herself would she admit that Ellis Pensford's anger might be the cause and determinedly put on an air of cheerfulness. 'A walk in the gardens would blow away our megrims,' she suggested.

They found Denvil Martin in the hall in the act of handing over a pair of rabbits to the butler. Looking up as the ladies descended the stairs, he came forward.

'Going out?' he enquired, 'if you'll give me a minute to return this to the gun-room, I'll join you, an I may.'

'You're up betimes,' observed Lyddie, eyeing his shooting jacket and muddy boots. 'Have you a headache to blow away like us?'

'Rather a feeling of restlessness, Lyddie.'

'Pining for the city life already, Denvil? I had thought better of you. It's such a short while since you joined us.'

'You know I came to comfort Grandmama with my presence when she didn't rally from Sir William's death as well as we hoped.'

Lydia laughed. 'I had thought it quite a different matter! I believed you retired to the country to—recuperate.'

'Have you been ill, Mr Martin?' asked Amy innocently with real concern and knew at once that she had made a mistake. Lyddie's smile changed into a muffled giggle and the gentleman's cheeks flushed a little as he looked away uneasily, but not before she had seen the flash of temper in his eyes.

'Nothing of the kind,' said Lyddie, overcoming her mirth. 'I was funning—you know how cousins tease.'

'Indeed, cousin Amy, you must know that Lyddie is a great one for playfulness,' Denvil, who appeared to have recovered himself, assured her. 'Pray don't take our chidings too seriously, believe me, no one else does.'

Amy found she didn't know how to answer this and, turning a little made a great show of flicking a speck of dust from the sleeve of her velvet spencer.

'Join us by the lake,' Lyddie said to her cousin, 'if you have to clean and oil that gun you'll be an age.'

'What did you mean, when you were talking to your cousin?' Amy asked curiously as she and Lyddie crossed the smooth, rolling lawns towards the lake.

The other girl glanced at her and laughed a little uncomfortably. 'Oh ... well I was being rather unkind, really—of course Grandmama doesn't guess, but Denvil is shockingly hard up. I don't know how for certain, but I believe the tradesmen were dunning him for money when he left London and he came here to gain a relief for a while. I shouldn't have teased him, but he's so pompous at times ... promise me that you'll not mention it to a soul and certainly not to my grandmother.'

Amy willingly gave her word and turned the matter thoughtfully over in her mind.

'It really must be quite dreadful to be poor,' went on her companion. 'Poor Denvil was cursed with a spendthrift for a father and by the time he died, most of Aunt Clarissa's dowry was gone.' Lydia took her friend's hand and held it in a warm grip. 'I know you were poor Amy, but you see, *he* has to keep up appearances. A gentleman could never admit to having his pockets to let.'

'Surely Lady Kingsclear would help him?'

'I'm sure she would, and has, but you see Grandpapa left the estate in such a way that she only has access to the interest. The capital and estate are left to his heirs and, of course, Denvil isn't one. Aunt Clarissa's father was Grandmama's first husband.'

'I see,' said Amy softly, feeling her way among this family tangle. 'Poor Denvil!'

'Just so—but not another word. Here he comes to join us.'

The talk about Lady Kingsclear's children had made Amy's thoughts return to her own parenthood and she was determined to tackle Jessie about the matter as she was certain that the maid knew a great deal more than she had so far admitted. The chance came later that day, when she took some flowers she had cut to Lady Kingsclear's room and found the elderly maid there alone, tidying some of her mistress's possessions.

'Good afternoon, Jessie,' the girl said brightly, wondering how to broach the subject. 'Have you a vase for these flowers I've brought for your mistress?'

Jessie glanced at the spray, assessing the size and height of the blossoms. 'There's a pewter jug on the windowsill,' she said, 'and a pitcher of water behind the screen in the corner.'

Amy filled the container and began

arranging the blooms. 'I think you said you've been here a long time?' she asked tentatively.

'Since I was a girl. I was sixteen when I came, miss.'

'And you've always been Lady Kingsclear's maid?'

Jessie snorted with derision. 'Love you, no, miss. I started as the still-room maid and worked my way up. I was nursemaid before I was personal maid, as I told you.'

Amy caught her breath at the opportunity presented. 'Tell me about Aubrey,' she said in a small voice and under her tense fingers one of the long stems snapped.

'Why are you so interested in Master Aubrey, if I might ask, miss?' Jessie asked slowly, her busy hands still among the linen she was folding.

Across the room Amy stared at the thin, angular back and took a shaking breath. 'I think you know—' she whispered and at her words the woman turned until their eyes met. 'I think I must—might be his daughter,' she said boldly, 'and I believe your mistress thinks so, too.'

The maid sat down suddenly and heavily. 'Never say so, miss,' she begged. 'M'lady lost her son years ago and it nearly killed her—she won't admit to having found his child until she's certain. If you wasn't who she suspects you are, it'ud break her heart anew.'

'But I have the right to know,' Amy pointed

out as calmly as she was able. 'Tell me about him, Jessie. How did she "lose" him?'

The older woman looked down at her work-worn hands clasped in her lap and, after a while, began to talk. 'He fell in love, miss and—after a terrible quarrel with his father, he ran away and we never saw anything more of him ... but we did hear later that he'd died...'

'Why did they quarrel? It must have been something dreadful to make them all so bitter.'

The maid compressed her lips. 'Twasn't suitable. A Kingsclear might be wild, but he's born a gentleman and it would never do for him to marry beneath himself.'

Amy's breath drifted out on a long sigh. 'So—he wanted to marry my mother.'

'They wouldn't have argued else, would they?' said the maid with all the servant's logic and remembering the ready acceptance of 'love children' Amy had to agree with her.

'And did they marry?' she asked, but Jessie grew cautious and would not say another word on that particular subject.

'If you'll take my advice, miss,' she said firmly, 'you'll put this matter out of your head for the time being. I've been with m'lady for a long time and I know that she doesn't like to be upset in any way, or have her plans put awry. At the moment she likes having you in the house and if you behave as she wants, I daresay she'll grow fond of you and it might be to your advantage—but annoy her, make her uncomfortable or unhappy and things won't go so well for you. Take my word for it.'

'Is her affection so transient, then?'

'She's had a hard life and over the years she's learned not to give her fondness too easily.' Jessie stood up and went back to her interrupted work. 'I'm sure you'll treat what I've said as a confidence, miss and not think I've been over bold in speaking clearly.'

Amy was to recall her words that evening after dinner. The ladies had retired to drink their tea and Denvil, with Ellis who had dined with them, had just joined them in the drawing-room, when Lady Kingsclear made her announcement.

'My dear Ellis,' she said calmly between sips from the delicate china cup she held. 'You'll be glad to know that I've taken your advice at last.'

'What advice was that, Aunt Charlie?' he asked, accepting a cup from Liddie and going to sit beside Lady Kingsclear.

'Why, you've told me, I don't know how many times, to make a new will and, at last, I've decided to attend to it. Mr Grey, Sir William's man of business, is coming to see me in the near future. I have some important details to change and a new bequest to make.'

Amy was uncomfortably aware that several pairs of eyes had followed the lady's glance towards herself and, biting her lips, flushed fiery red under their concerted gaze. Across the room Medora stared at her, her eyes wide with an angry challenge. Lydia gazed at her thoughtfully a half smile in her eyes, while Denvil Martin had grown suddenly still, the quizzing glass he had been idly toying with suspended, swaying from his hand.

Captain Pensford's expression was inscrutable, carefully schooled to betray nothing, but Amy found herself shivering under the cold, grey gaze which seemed to hold a faint but definite air of menace. At last he looked away from her, turning back to his aunt to say easily,

'You must do as you wish, Aunt, but pray allow me to advise you to be swayed by Mr Grey, who has always had your interests at heart.' Again he glanced at Amy and she found herself unable to meet his eyes and his gaze travelled on to his cousin. 'Denvil, a game of cards?' he suggested softly. 'To play at chance would suit me very well tonight, but be warned, I have my hand and eye in, and will see through any tricks or knavery you care to try in a flash.'

CHAPTER SIX

Afterwards, Amy was never sure when the revelation came to her; perhaps she awoke with the knowledge, only realising later that she possessed it, or maybe the realisation dawned

95

on her slowly. Whenever it was, the fact suddenly came to her mind, hitting her almost with the force of a blow, making her grasp and clutch the dressing table to still her reeling brain.

Thankful that she was alone, Amy stared back at her wide-eyed reflection, while she strove to assimilate the knowledge that filled her with a growing excitement, while she tried to define the wild emotions that shook her.

Slowly she sank onto a stool, one hand pressed against her thudding heart while she tried to accept that if her parents had married, no matter how lowly the situation of her mother, then she was the heir to Kingsclear Court. Such a fact explained a great many things; Lady Kingsclear's reluctance to acknowledge her until her parentage was certain, Medora's ready dislike, Captain Pensford's hostility—even Denvil Martin's wary friendship. All could be explained if it was presumed that she might be the heiress, usurping the position of the two accepted granddaughters.

Suddenly the bedchamber was small and oppressive. Although the sky was overcast and heavy with rain, on impulse Amy dragged on her riding habit, snatched up her gloves and hat and ran from the room, down the back stairs and out to the stables. Even Lyddie's company would have been unwelcome at that moment and she curtly refused the services of the young groom who would have ridden with her, telling him that she did not mean to leave the park.

Riding, which had been such a fearful activity a few weeks ago, had progressed to a pleasant experience and, although a novice and inexperienced, Amy found that she enjoyed her habitual morning canters through the grounds that surrounded the Court.

Several rides had been cut through the trees that formed a small wood in the furthest corner of the park and she had just turned back from the high wall that bounded Kingsclear Court, when an approaching horseman caught her eyes and she turned in the saddle the better to see who was bent on joining her.

'Good morning, Miss Clear,' said Ellis Pensford, touching the brim of his curly beaver with the tip of his riding crop. 'I was told I would find you here.'

Amy lifted her eyebrows. 'Indeed?' she said coolly, 'I had no idea that my movements were so well known.'

'I believe that you will find that I know a very great deal.'

Staring back at him, Amy felt her temper begin to smoulder a little as his cool regard travelled slowly, almost insolently, over her.

'I presume you intend to give me one of your usual setdowns,' she cried, for once forgetting the usual inward trepidation the soldier roused in her.

97

'Indeed I do, Miss,' he said, the words clipped and short. 'An you remember, I told you that I would allow you to stay here as long as it pleased my aunt—'

'And have I displeased Lady Kingsclear?' Amy demanded but the man ignored her question and went on.

'And disturbed no one else,' he finished inexorably. 'Kingsclear Court used to be a calm, tranquil house—'

'You must be talking about since Sir William died,' interrupted Amy between her teeth. 'From all I hear it was far more lively before.'

'Did no one teach you the rudiments of good manners?' Captain Pensford asked, at last deigning to acknowledge her outbursts.

Amy laughed on a brittle note. 'Alas, no one told me that manners were a requisite for an adventuress!' she mourned. 'Had I realised, you may be sure I would have studied them.'

Ellis Pensford's mouth tightened visibly. 'You'd be wise not to provoke me,' he warned.

'I quite understand how easy it would be to hide a body under these trees,' Amy told him. 'And of course any queries would be turned away with all the ease with which this family usually deals with questions.'

Deciding to ignore this interesting sally, the soldier went on, watching her reaction intently while he spoke. 'My man returned from Portsmouth this morning.'

98

Her eyes flew to his face and the fluctuating colour danced in her cheeks, but he was unable to decide if she was dismayed or eager. Outwardly impassive he waited for her to question him, refusing to add to his statement until she spoke.

Amy stared at him, one part of her even aware of how handsome he was in the dappled sunlight that filtered between the leafy branches overhead, while her mind searched for the meaning behind his flatly stated announcement.

'And—what news did he bring?' she asked at last.

'Much, concerning you,' he answered, his grey gaze still holding her.

Her hand tightened on the reins and sensing her tenseness the little mare cavorted restlessly, making her harness jingle in the silence.

'Is this news to be another of your secrets—or am I to learn what it might be?'

'It's no secret, Miss Clear. He found your entry in the register at the orphanage—but you were handed in by an elderly man who gave his name as Ward and who said he was your guardian.'

Trees and grass spun round Amy. 'No!' she cried. 'No—I remember my mother—'

'You may have told yourself stories,' Ellis said gently. 'Children often do.'

'No—I *remember* her. I have no recollection of an old man. The entry must be wrong.'

99

'I fear there is no possibility of that.'

'There must be,' she could only repeat heedless of the tears that filled her eyes as she faced him. 'Don't—take all I have—from me,' she faltered, her expression almost pleading.

The Captain's face was enigmatic, but his tone was adamant. 'An you remember, I warned you to give up this scheme of yours before you were hurt . . . be sure I'll find out the truth of this matter.' For a moment he stared down at her pale face. 'You'd have done better to remain a governess,' he told her harshly.

With a hand that shook slightly, Amy dashed the tears from her cheeks. 'I h-have not been idle these last weeks,' she remarked in a voice that trembled only a little. 'You may be surprised to learn that I have discovered that I am almost certainly the daughter of Lady Kingsclear's only son—' She shot him a quick glance, but he remained silent, his eyes clear and cold in his carefully schooled face. 'And, if that is so—and my parents were married, as I believe they were . . . then, Captain Pensford, I am heir to Kingsclear Court.'

The words died on her lips and hung on the air between their mounts. She had not meant to say so much, his attitude had goaded her into telling him far more than she had intended. A quick glance told her that he was still regarding her intently and she unconsciously braced her shoulders and lifted her chin a little, regardless of the drying tear tracks on her cheeks.

'You'll have to prove it, miss—and can you do that?'

Facing him the girl raised her eyes to his. 'I'll do my best,' she told him quietly.

'Give up, Miss Clear,' he urged. 'I have no wish to hurt you—but I will have no qualms if it comes either to you or anyone of the Kingsclears.'

Amy shivered a little. 'Even if I am one of them?'

'Have you anything to substantiate your claim?'

'My—looks. Even you say I resemble the family.'

Ignoring the air of pleading, Ellis shook his head, smiling somewhat grimly. 'The Kingsclear banner is no sign of legitimacy,' he told her curtly.

'There is a portrait of Aubrey—'

'Still no surety of being born on the right side of the blanket.'

Amy flushed at his words, aware that he was deliberately baiting her and searched her mind for some other sign that the man beside her would find acceptable. 'There's—my Bible,' she offered at last.

'Aha—we are back to the beginnings now. I'd like to see this signature of yours ... it would undoubtedly prove interesting.'

'Then you shall,' she said impulsively goaded by his air of amused doubt. 'Come to the house and I'll show it to you.'

101

Ellis allowed himself to be mildly interested. 'You have it with you?'

'Indeed, I have. I brought it with me.'

'How foresighted of you,' the soldier remarked, 'but it will have to wait—'

'No—now!' she insisted, her eyes shining with excitement, 'or have you no wish to be confronted with such evidence?'

His eyebrows quirked. 'A challenge?' he queried and made up his mind. 'Very well—I'll come and see this proof of yours, but this afternoon will have to suffice—I have a meeting with my bailiff arranged for this morning.' He tipped his hat negligently with one finger. 'Shall we say three o'clock, then?' he stated rather than asked and, turning his mount, rode off, leaving Amy in a state of indecision.

Watching his straight back as he cantered away from her, she wondered at her turmoil of emotions, uncertain whether anger or excitement were foremost. Uneasily she stared along the broad length of the tree-lined ride at the diminishing figure before, jerking her reins, she turned and headed rapidly towards the house.

Leaving the little mare in the care of the groom, she entered the house by the way she had left and was met by a maidservant in a great state of suppressed excitement.

'Miss Lyddie sent me to find you, miss,' she said, 'and to ask you to come to the servant's

102

hall. There's a gipsy pedlar woman called, with a pack of lace and ribbons and "lucks" to buy.'

Amy smiled. 'Indeed, I must see her. Give me time to run upstairs to find my purse and I'll join Miss Lyddie in the hall.'

She found the woman seated by the open fire, a tankard of beer on the table by her elbow and an open sack at her feet. Glittering black eyes looked up at her approach and the girl felt a momentary chill run uneasily down her spine at the inscrutable gaze. Luxuriant, wild hair was half confined beneath a knotted scarf, a dirty white blouse was tucked into the waist of a full scarlet skirt that fell in thick folds to the floor almost covering the gipsy's bare brown feet. Amy wondered at her age, only knowing that the woman had left her youth behind and yet was obviously still well aware of her almost animal attraction.

White teeth showed between the red lips as the gipsy smiled. 'Come nearer, lady,' she said in a husky voice. 'I've laces and ribbons and gewgaws aplenty.'

She made an inviting gesture towards the sack on the floor and Amy dragged her fascinated eyes away from the colourful figure, suddenly aware that Lyddie was examining a bundle spread out on the table and that several of the servants were crowded expectantly around.

The woman took a clay pipe from her waist band and reaching forward, thrust a spill

103

between the bars of the fire and lit the tobacco already in the tiny bowl. A sweet pungent scent unlike any other tobacco Amy had ever smelt, began to fill the hall and almost against her will, Amy took a step towards the waiting figure.

'She says she'll tell our fortunes,' said Lyddie, looking over her shoulder. 'And really this lace is very pleasant. 'Twill do admirably to trim our underthings. Do come and see, I've put the best aside.'

Aware of the black, enigmatic gaze that had watched her since she entered, the other girl reluctantly began to sort through the tangled mass, selecting some lengths and then turning her attention to the gay ribbons that Lydia was holding.

As she held out a coin to the gipsy, her hand was taken in a hard grip. Despite her quick withdrawal, her hand was turned over and her fingers straightened out to reveal her palm. For a few seconds the woman gazed at it intently, while the smoke from her pipe drifted up between them, making the girl's eyes smart and her breath catch in her throat.

'You're looking for something, lady,' she began after a while in a curious flat voice. 'I see a search that will end where three white ladies stand...' She paused and began to rock herself to and fro. After a while she went on, but now her tone was sweet and crooning. 'I see water— and one who would do you harm ... secrets

104

and mystery and black deeds. Take care where you love—for friends can be enemies and nothing as you suspect. I see a book with a name on it—a man—hair wet with water and a dress green with weeds...'

With a jerk Amy pulled her hand free. 'Enough!' she cried, staring down into the sunburned face with something very like revulsion before she gave a brittle laugh and tried to hide the unease the words had roused in her by saying lightly, 'An you must tell me my fortune, I would rather hear something to my advantage.'

Opaque eyes stared back. 'I tell the truth, lady,' said the gipsy, but now her voice was normal. 'Take heed of what I say...' Suddenly losing interest in the girl, she looked round and asked impatiently if anyone else wished to hear what the future held.

Lyddie knelt by her feet and willingly surrendered her palm for her scrutiny. Black eyes searched her face and the woman smiled, relaxing against the table at her back. 'You have a lucky face, lady,' she said. 'And a life to go with it. You'll marry well and have a family of children to care for you in your old age. I see love and happiness for you.'

'That's not very exciting,' laughed Lyddie, 'can't you promise me anything more dramatic?'

Above her head the gipsy looked at Amy. 'Take what you have, lady,' she advised briskly, 'and don't wish for wild things. There's some will have excitement aplenty and wish they hadn't.'

'I vow it was as good as a play,' giggled Lyddie as the girls climbed the stairs to their rooms. 'Your face—your eyes grew as big as moons as the gipsy dame went on. Do you believe her? You looked quite frightened.'

'I'd have preferred it if she had told me a farrago such as she told you. I'd much liefer have a lovely life, than this one of mystery and excitement the gipsy dame has set out for me— and a wet ending.'

Involuntarily she shivered and Lyddie pulled her arm through her own. ''Twas only fun,' she protested, 'and not to be believed. Surely you don't think she could really tell the future? I have it on the best authority that these pedlar folk question the servants and villagers to find out all the gossip before they offer to read our palms.'

'It's strange though,' murmured the other girl thoughtfully. 'She knew so much ... even about my Bible with Lady Kingsclear's name in it.'

'She could have heard it all from the servants,' comforted Lydia. 'It is surprising how much they know about us, even when we think we've been discreet.' She paused at the entrance to Amy's room. 'Come along to my chamber when you've changed your habit and we'll show Medora our purchases.' She smiled hesitantly at the other girl. 'I'd like you two to be friends, you know,' she said, faintly wistful.

'I'll do my best,' Amy promised readily, 'but I don't feel that she is very keen.'

Later when she entered Lyddie's room and the golden haired sister looked up with an expressionless face and antagonistic eyes, she sighed inwardly, but nevertheless smiled a little and offered to show the lace she had bought.

'Lyddie has already displayed hers,' she was told. 'And one is much like another.'

'Why didn't you come down to the servant's hall?' asked her sister quickly.

'I find buying cheap material a false economy—one is forever replacing them.'

'But, she wasn't only selling ribbons and laces,' observed Amy quietly, 'she told our fortunes, too.'

Medora looked up quickly, a spark of interest in her blue eyes. 'Indeed? Why did you not tell me, Lyddie? I would like to know what the future held—not of course that I believe in such things. In this scientific age such old superstitions are only for the uneducated and lower classes.'

'Well, I for one have every intention of believing my fortune. She told me I'd marry a wealthy husband and have lots of children.'

Medora gave a short laugh. 'How vastly original, Lyddie dear! And how cosy. Couldn't she have thought of anything more exciting?'

'I rather believe she expended all her

107

imagination on me and had none to spare for other people.'

Staring at Amy, the older sister raised her thin eyebrows. 'You intrigue me, Miss Clear. Pray what does the future have in store for you? Not a wealthy match and a quiverful of offspring?'

'Nothing so mundane,' said Amy. 'Rather mystery and secret enemies—and a watery end of some kind.'

Medora's eyes opened wide as she considered the girl seated on the window-seat. 'How—entertaining,' she said at last, 'but we all know that you are a female of secrets. If this gipsy woman knew your origins 'twould have been only kind to share the knowledge with us. I, for one, would be interested to know what—'

'It was a great pity that you didn't come with us,' interrupted Lydia. 'She might have been able to say where your bracelet is.'

'Oh, don't mention it,' sighed Medora, diverted. 'Grandmama has given me such a scold and I vow my chamber has been turned upside down. I feel quite fatigued and have searched my memory until my poor brain reels and the very thought of it gives me the megrims.'

'You should have put it away,' her sister said unsympathetically and at once Medora rounded on her, her eyes flashing with anger.

'I daresay—so everyone loses no time in telling me and I'll give you no thanks for

108

joining their ranks, Lydia. You'd best remember that there are things that we'd all better not do, and not act so pie with me, miss.'

Lyddie shrugged slightly and turned away to Amy. 'Shall we ask for the carriage this afternoon and pay a call on some neighbours?'

'I would have liked that above all, but,' she coloured a little in confusion but went on bravely, 'but, Captain Pensford is coming to see me after lunch.'

Her announcement startled both her listeners. Medora making no secret of her surprise and incredulous interest, while even Lyddie looked faintly curious.

'Why, pray, should our cousin be calling on you?' demanded the blonde girl.

'I don't believe that is our business,' observed her sister quietly. 'If Amy wishes us to know then she will tell us no doubt.'

'Of course it's our business,' replied Medora crossly. 'Ellis is our kinsman and she—she is a nobody, living here on sufferance and charity.'

'I have no objection to you knowing,' said Amy. 'Indeed, Lydia already knows that I have a Bible with Lady Kingsclear's signature in it—Ellis is merely coming to view it.'

'*Captain Pensford* if you please, miss,' snapped Medora pettishly, 'you are over familiar.'

'And you are ridiculous!' cried her sister. 'Grandmama told us to term Amy "cousin" and if we may call her so, then she may be free with our names.'

Medora hunched a shoulder, covered in an elegant sleeve and looked challengingly at Amy. 'I shall be vastly interested in this book,' she said coldly. 'You may be sure that I shall view it as avidly as Ellis. I vow we are sadly in need of entertainment.'

'Who am I to deny you entertainment? I shall be pleased to show it to anyone who cares to be in the library at three of the clock this afternoon.'

Having made her statement Amy felt obliged to keep to it, however she was a little discomposed to find not only Lyddie and Medora waiting her, but Denvil standing nonchalantly behind the settee on which they were seated. She hesitated a little under their concerted stare before closing the door behind her, she encountered an encouraging smile from Lyddie and advanced into the room, only too aware of the interest centred on the wooden box she carried.

'I see no book,' said Medora, her voice sharp.

'Be sure I have it,' the other said calmly. ''Tis locked away for safety in this box.'

'Oh, Amy,' cried Lyddie impulsively, starting to her feet, 'are you sure you want us here? If our presence embarrasses you, we'll gladly leave.'

Amy smiled at her. 'Please stay,' she said, 'I feel in need of a friend.'

Lyddie touched her hand and sat down again, just as the door opened and the butler announced Captain Pensford. For a moment he, too, stood in the doorway while he surveyed the occupants of the room, then as the door was closed by Wilkins, he came easily forward.

'Ladies,' he said a little formally with a slight bow, 'Denvil. I must confess that I had not expected to find such a gathering.'

'La, Ellis, once the secret was out, do you suppose that we would have stayed away?'

Grey eyes found Amy. 'Was it a secret, Miss Clear?' he asked. 'I had not supposed it so.'

'Lyddie knew—I would have spoken about it, had the opportunity arose.'

'Exactly so,' he said and strode forward to the table where she had set the box and stood looking down at the inlaid surface. One slim brown finger briefly touched its decorated lid and for a moment a puzzled frown drew his black brows together.

'Pray, cousin don't keep us in suspense,' cried Medora. 'Open it and show us this important signature.'

With the briefest of glances at Ellis, Amy reached forward, turned the tiny key already in the lock and raised the lid with a decisive gesture. As the contents came into view, her face lost all its animation as she stared blankly down, her hand suspended.

'There is no book,' declaimed Medora on a

111

note of triumph. 'Did I not suspect so all day?'

Watching Ellis's and Amy's faces intently Denvil made a gesture for silence and slowly rose to his feet, while Lyddie went to her friend's side and, in her turn, looked down into the open box.

Amy shut her eyes, both hands gripping the edge of the table so tightly that her knuckles showed white. 'I had no idea—' she whispered. 'You must believe me that I didn't know it was there.'

'What is it?' demanded Medora, agog with curiosity and joined the others at the table. 'My bracelet!' she screeched and snatched it up, rounding on Amy. 'You took it,' she accused furiously. 'You are the thief—well be sure Grandmama will hear of this.'

Amy half made a small, pleading gesture, but at the venom in the other's eyes, her hand fell hopelessly to her side as she looked round at the others. 'Truly, I didn't take it,' she said, her face drained of colour.

Above Lydia's bent head, her eyes sought those of Ellis and she stared up at him, quite unaware of the pleading her expression held. Unconsciously she put out her hand and felt her arm taken in his strong grip as he put her into a chair.

'Medora,' he said crisply, 'sit down and be quiet. You always were excitable as a child and I see that age has not improved you.' His eyes found his cousin. 'Denvil, if you would be so

112

good—' He waited until Medora had been led back to the settee, before turning back to the chair where Amy sat with Lyddie by her side.

'I take it that Medora had lost this bracelet?'

'The night of our dance,' his cousin told him. 'She neglected to return it to Grandmama for safe keeping and it could not be found in the morning.'

Grey eyes studied Amy's pale face. 'You knew of this?'

'Yes—but I—'

His cool voice cut across her. 'And the house has been searched?'

Medora answered. 'The maids looked everywhere in my room, and the corridors and hall—no one would have thought of looking in the other bedchambers. We forgot that we housed a foundling and one not used to being trusted.'

'Medora—you are unkind,' protested Lyddie. 'I am sure there is some explanation.'

'Let us be calm and civilised and discuss this matter in a sensible manner,' suggested Denvil. 'Cousin Amy, can you suggest how the bracelet came to be in your box?'

Amy shook her head miserably and twisted her hands together in the lap of her muslin dress.

Above her head Ellis spoke. 'And you kept the box—where?'

'In my room on a table by the bed.'

'You opened it with a key, I remember.

113

Where did you keep the key?'

She stared at him hopelessly. 'In the lock,' she confessed, struck with her own folly.

'Not very sensible,' he suggested a little sardonically.

'But very useful—in the circumstances,' put in Medora viciously.

Captain Pensford turned to survey her through his quizzing glass. 'You are uncharitable,' he told her. 'It seems unlikely to me that if Amy had put the missing bracelet in the box, she would have brought it down so readily for all of us to see.'

For a second Medora stared back at him, before her eyes fell beneath his steady gaze. 'She—could have forgotten,' she offered.

'I doubt it,' her cousin said calmly. 'I think that whoever put the bracelet there, it was not Miss Clear.'

Silence greeted his words, then a babble of conversation broke out as Medora wildly made accusations which Lydia hotly denied while Denvil did his best to calm them both. Only Ellis and Amy were quiet and, suddenly aware of his intent gaze, she looked up, shyly aware of his unexpected championship.

While she watched he went across to his cousin and bent to speak in his ear. Denvil nodded understandingly and a moment later, ushered Medora and Lydia out of the room.

'And now we come to our business. I have not yet seen the signature we spoke of.'

114

Amy gestured to the small, leather-bound book in the box and watched as he took it to the window the better to examine it.

'Thank you for—defending me,' she said half hesitantly.

Ellis raised his head. 'You mistake the matter, Miss Clear,' he replied. 'I had no intention of defending anyone, but rather spoke as I believed the affair to stand. It would have been exceedingly foolish on your part to bring the evidence down in the box for all to see ... and whatever I believe you to be, it is not a simpleton.'

Amy's gaze wavered and fell beneath his hard eyes as the ready colour painfully stained her cheeks. After a moment the soldier returned his attention to the volume in his hands. At last he closed the cover, standing for a few seconds staring out at the trim lawns and sparkling lake before turning back into the room, his eyes fell on the girl and his expression became extremely thoughtful.

Crossing to her, he dropped her property in her lap and continued on his way to the door.

'But ... my book ... Lady Kingsclear's signature!' Amy stammered, starting to her feet. 'What do you think of it?'

One hand on the door handle, Ellis turned back to face her. 'Very little, Coz,' he said coolly. 'The words might read Charlotte Kingsclear, but I must tell you, an you don't know, that the writing is very clearly not that of my aunt. I cannot imagine that you would be so naive as to suppose that I would not be acquainted with Lady Kingsclear's signature and so am hard put to find some explanation for your conduct,' and, with the curtest of bows, he was gone.

CHAPTER SEVEN

Left alone, Amy had stared blankly at the closed door, clutching the Bible against her bosom with both hands, scarcely aware of what she was doing. Becoming aware of the object between her hands, she glanced down at it, bewilderment in her eyes, before running quietly out of the library to her own room.

Raised voices carried to her from the drawing-room as she passed, Medora's shrill tones sounding high and agitated, but the girl hurried on with scarcely a pause, seeking the sanctity of her bedchamber. Turning the key in the lock, she crossed to the window and stood staring out at the smooth lawn and sparkling lake for some time.

At last she turned and taking her carpetbag from a cupboard began to search feverishly among its contents until she found the letter Lady Kingsclear had written to her. Taking it to the window, she compared the two ... and had to admit Captain Pensford had been right; the name and similarity of style had deceived her. Looking at them now in the new light presented to her, Amy wondered how she could ever have thought them the same and knew in her heart that she had allowed herself to believe what she wanted to be the truth.

Sighing, she put the letter and book away, her fingers lingering a little as she smoothed worn leather and involuntarily came the question, who had been the unknown Charlotte?

Busy with the complexity of her thoughts, the hours sped by and she was startled to realise that the afternoon was over, when she raised her heavy eyes at a gentle tap on her door.

'It's me—Lyddie. May I come in?'

Amy unlocked the door and stood back wordlessly as her friend entered. For a moment they stared at each other, then Lyddie smiled.

'Don't look so fierce,' she said. 'We are all agreed that the thief must have hidden the bracelet in your box until such time as it was safe to recover it.'

'Even Medora?'

There was a pause and Lyddie looked away uncomfortably. After a while the other girl sighed and announced a little defiantly that she intended to make the affair known to Lady Kingsclear.

'I have already done so—I thought I would present the matter in the fairest light. Grandmama was very understanding and now wishes the business closed—except for endeavouring to find out who was responsible, of course.'

'Could it have been one of the servants?' asked Amy diffidently. 'Perhaps taking it by mistake and then realising what they had done ... and dropping it in my box as the nearest hiding place.'

'It must have been something like that,' soothed her friend. 'We will say no more but forget the whole thing. I came to tell you that it was time to get dressed for dinner.'

Amy moved restlessly, glancing out at the lengthening shadows. 'I had not realised that it was so late.'

'I wondered if you intended to come to table,' Lyddie said delicately. 'Grandmama wanted me to tell you that she is taking dinner with us ... I believe that she wishes you to be present.'

Amy assured her that she had every intention of being in the dining-room that evening, but the thought of facing the members of the Kingsclear family who had so lately been her accusers, made her heartbeat quicken with nervousness. Putting on her best dinner gown of lemon crepe to bolster her courage, she took especial care over her hair and dabbled lavishly with perfume.

Entering the drawing-room with her head held high, she encountered the eyes turned in her direction and tried to keep her countenance as she read the divided emotions facing her. Medora's blue eyes were blazing antagonism, encouragement showed behind Lyddie's kind smile. Denvil's carefully schooled gaze held nothing beyond a polite interest, while Ellis's lazy grey eyes held an expression that might have been reluctant admiration.

'La,' came Medora's shrill tones, 'we had not expected you tonight, Miss Clear.'

'Come and sit by me,' commanded a softer voice and Amy looked beyond the younger people to where Lady Kingsclear reclined on a settee.

Thankful for her kindness, she crossed the room and sank down beside her. The older woman reached across and patted her hand.

'I hear you paid a visit to the gipsy this morning,' she said. 'Of course it's not the same now and you young folk have more to entertain you than I had in my day, but I remember well the excitement occasioned when a pedlar called at the kitchen door when I was a girl.'

The awkward moment was smoothed over and thanks to Lady Kingsclear's management the evening passed without mention of the subject uppermost in the diners' minds.

With so much to occupy her thoughts Amy spent a restless night, climbing thankfully out of her tumbled bed as soon as she heard the servants moving. Pulling on a cotton wrap, she pushed back the curtains and, opening a

119

casement, leaned her heavy head against the cool glass as a gentle breeze caressed her hot cheeks.

A mist hung over the garden, drifting like smoke over the terrace and around the trees and shrubs. As she watched two figures emerged briefly like dimly seen ghosts before the swirling mist hid them again. Interested inspite of her preoccupation, Amy watched to see if they would appear again, but when after a few minutes the haze lifted again the place where they had been was empty.

Puzzled, Amy continued to stare at the damp garden. The long red skirt she had glimpsed could only have belonged to the gipsy woman, while the tall figure in a blue coat beside her, bending close in confidence and with his head hidden by the shadow of a black beaver had been unrecognisable.

The mist gave way to a brilliant sun that soon dried the dew on the grass and made everyone restless to be out of doors.

'A picnic luncheon by the lake is just the thing,' declaimed Lydia. 'If you'll write a note for Ellis, Medora, I'll arrange the meal.'

'He won't come,' put in Denvil. 'I heard him telling Grandmama that he was spending the morning with his bailiff—something to do with those new cottages he's putting up for his workers.'

Medora pouted. 'I vow cousin Ellis spends more time with his tenants than he does with us! It's too bad of him.'

'Shall we ask Grandmama to take luncheon with us?' asked Lyddie. 'She might enjoy it.'

'I doubt it,' said her sister. 'The distance will be too far or the heat too great. You know how she dislikes the effort of such things.'

'Perhaps you'd ask her, Amy?' smiled Lyddie and Denvil offered to arrange the picnic site as the girls left the room.

To her surprise Amy's invitation was readily accepted, Lady Kingsclear's door being firmly barred to visitors at so early an hour, but Jessie readily carrying the messages. The maid stepped out herself just as Amy was leaving. 'I'll go and see myself that the sedan chair is in readiness. It's kept in the coach house and I know it's what m'lady uses on such occasions,' she said.

The girl looked up at the tall, angular figure in the dark, print dress and asked a question that had been troubling her for some time. 'Jessie—do you know who it was that Aubrey Kingsclear ran away with?'

Jessie stopped, pausing a moment before turning slowly towards the girl behind her. 'What a question, miss ... may I ask what it's to do with you?' she said tartly.

'Oh, Jessie—just tell me. *Please*.'

Something in Amy's voice made the other's expression soften slightly and the girl pressed home her advantage quickly.

'Was she a servant here?'

121

'Nothing like—she was Mr Berridge, the vicar's daughter,' and as though she had said more than she should and had no intention of adding anything further, Jessie closed her mouth and turned on her heel and marched away.

All morning Amy hugged the knowledge to herself. Until then she had imagined that her mother was one of the servants, which readily explained the Kingsclear's aversion to the affair between the girl and Sir William's only son. She had not been prepared for the aristocrat's dislike of a match between his heir and the vicar's daughter, until she realised all the ambitions that were centred on the marriage of an only son.

The alfresco meal proved to be a success, even Medora forgetting her grievances enough to join in the conversation that was general as they relaxed after the picnic.

'What a pleasant park, you have, Grandmama,' she remarked, leaning back against the cushions and spreading her parasol to shade her face. 'One forgets, living in London, the delights of owning a garden.'

Lady Kingsclear was amused. 'I am sure, if you ask your Papa, he will allow you to stay here—but the autumn is not far away and of course the Season will soon begin...'

'Grandmama,' protested Medora quickly, 'I would never dream of foisting myself upon you for such a length of time. I vow you have been goodness itself in having us here, but we all know the effort involved—'

'Have no fear, Medora,' Lady Kingsclear said dryly. 'I shan't keep you here too long.'

'We like being here,' put in Lydia quietly. 'Summer wouldn't be the same spent anywhere but at Kingsclear Court.' She and her grandmother exchanged smiles and then she went on reminiscently. 'Do you remember the year Grandpapa determined to clean the lake and re-stock it with fish?'

'Indeed, I do. Such a fuss and bother all to no avail for the fish all took something and died and the bottom of the lake was so foul that I thought we'd all die of putrid sore throats.'

'We used to play on the little island in the middle,' added Denvil lazily chewing a blade of grass. 'You girls made believe that the tastefully ruined temple was a house.'

Amy looked across at the little man-made island overgrown with trees and grass. Suddenly her eyes narrowed. 'Surely—that *can't* be people,' she cried staring at a group of dimly seen figures, half hidden by greenery.

'No—statues,' supplied Lyddie.

'But, I've never seen them before.'

'I believe they can only be seen from this position.'

Denvil frowned. 'What did we call them? I recall that we had some outlandish name for them.'

'The White Ladies,' supplied his

123

grandmother with a laugh. 'You made up some story that they were three of our Nuns turned to stone for some horrid misdeed.'

'The Three White Ladies,' mused Medora, unaware of the effect her words had upon Amy. 'What games we played centred around those marble maidens.'

The conversation flowed on, but Amy was silent trying to recall exactly what the gipsy had said. Thoughtfully she stared across the stretch of water to where the marble statues gleamed in the bright sunshine. Suddenly, from a dearth of information about her possible parentage, she had two clues to follow. True, the gipsy's prophecy was not to be regarded seriously but all the same she decided to pay the isle a visit if she was able and in the meanwhile she determined to seek out the vicar of the nearby village of Boxdean.

From the visits she had paid to the church with the family on Sundays, she knew that Mr Berridge was no longer rector, but she had hopes that the incumbent might have news of his predecessor and set about finding an excuse to call upon him at the earliest possible moment.

The task was easier than she had expected; the afternoon after the picnic by the lake, Lady Kingsclear sent for her and asked her to deliver a bundle of pencils to Mrs Ford, the Vicar's wife for use in the Sunday school she ran.

Amy truthfully professed herself delighted

124

to run the errand and, pausing only to tie a straw bonnet over her gleaming hair, set off at once.

Once outside the high walls of the park, she took the lane between thick hedgerows that led to the village, revelling in the sense of freedom she felt. For almost the first time since coming to the Court, she was alone, and choosing to ignore the nagging knowledge that Lady Kingsclear would have expected her to take a maid even though the road to Boxdean was short.

Soon the village came into sight and Amy lingered by the tiny shop, peering in the small window at the treasures laid out, before she went on, passing the church and turning in at the narrow gate to the new, stone vicarage.

Mrs Ford was pleased to see her and, mindful that the Kingsclears held the living of Boxdean, treated Amy with all the deferent courtesy due to a member of that family.

'Miss Clear has come to call,' she said to her husband, rousing that gentleman from the depths of a new sermon he was writing. 'Is it not kind of her ladyship to take the trouble of sending the school pencils?'

'It was no trouble,' Amy assured her, wondering how she could advance the subject that had brought her to the vicarage.

'You'll take a dish of tea?' asked Mrs Ford and bustled away to supervise the setting out of the tray.

Silence fell in the little parlour. Mr Ford's thoughts evidently still with the planning of next Sunday's sermon and Amy endeavouring to find a topic that might interest him. At last she took a deep breath and asked, almost without intending it, if he had known Mr Berridge.

'Berridge? I fancy I have heard it,' the vicar was puzzled.

'He was incumbent here about twenty years ago.'

'That's a long time,' he observed, a twinkle at the back of his eyes, 'but I do recall the name, now.' Closing his eyes he rubbed his lined forehead with an ink-stained finger.

'Do you happen to know where he went when he left here?'

Opening surprisingly astute eyes, he looked at her for a moment. 'It is of importance?'

'To me.'

'Then, give me a moment—I remember my predecessor saying that he had gone to a village not far distant ... but surely you could ask at the Court? After all they have the dispensation of the living in their hands.'

'I—find that I am unable to ask Lady Kingsclear,' Amy confessed in a low voice, 'and so I would be grateful if you could help me.'

For a little longer, the vicar held her gaze. 'I believe I might have the information among the church papers,' he said at last and excused himself just as his wife and a maid carrying a large tray appeared.

Not until the tea was drunk and Amy on the point of leaving, did he reappear, dropping a slip of paper into her hand as she took her leave of him. Amy smiled her thanks as she slipped it into her reticule and then hurried down the path and out of the village, not pausing until she was out of sight of the houses and could read the address without fear of being observed.

'The Vicarage, St Paul's in the Fields, Alford,' she read and tucked it back into her bag, feeling that at last the mystery of her parentage was within her grasp.

The way back to the Court seemed to have lengthened since she trod that way earlier that afternoon. The heat from the late afternoon sun was almost unendurable and, after a careful scrutiny of her surroundings to make sure she was unseen, with great daring Amy pulled off her bonnet and carried it by its strings, loosening the curl's from her hot head. Even her thin muslin gown seemed to hold the heat and she thought wistfully of the tales she had heard of fashionable ladies who dampened their dresses to make them cling more closely.

In the deep well of the lane, the sun beat down unmercifully with not a whisper of wind to stir the hedgerows. With each step her slippers scuffed up little spurts of dry dust, which penetrated her white stockings and crept

127

uncomfortably between her toes.

At last, tired and tried beyond all measure, she climbed up onto a stile that was placed invitingly under a patch of shade cast by a huge oak and sat there fanning herself with the brim of her modish bonnet, while she recovered a little.

Intent on watching a butterfly that was fluttering its wings on the leaf of a nearby flower, she did not hear the sound of an approaching horse, looking up startled only when it was a few yards distant. Hastily sliding off her perch, she smoothed her narrow skirts, unhappily aware that she had been showing a great deal more of her ankle than Lady Kingsclear would have deemed ladylike.

'Miss Clear—Amy,' said Denvil Martin, viewing her from his saddle. 'What do you here—and alone?'

'I have been on an errand for Lady Kingsclear.'

'But without a companion—did you take no maid with you? I cannot believe that she would have left you to walk home alone.'

Amy lifted her chin. 'I saw no need.'

Denvil was scandalised. 'Lydia and Medora are always accompanied.'

'Mr Martin, you forget that I am an orphanage miss and not used to the niceties enjoyed by your cousins. In Portsmouth, which I venture to believe considerably more dangerous than here, I was used to walk

128

alone—accompanied at most by a child of twelve.' She looked around at the peaceful scene and smiled up at him. 'Surely no harm can come to me here?'

Swinging himself from the back of his horse, he offered her his arm and gathered the reins in his free hand. 'I'll allow that it would appear so, cousin,' he admitted. 'But convention demands that young ladies should be chaperoned and I know that Lady Kingsclear would not be easy in her mind if she supposed you to be walking about the countryside alone.'

'Must I replace my bonnet also?' Amy asked demurely, a hint of mischief in her voice.

'I believe it's customary for ladies of quality to cover their heads outside the house, but as we are ... cousins and alone, I imagine that such conventions may be overlooked under the circumstances.'

Darting a fleeting glance at him, Amy encountered such an intent look from him that her own gaze fell and she thought wildly that she had forgotten that Mr Martin had a penchant for flirting. His next action confirmed her suspicions; reaching out, he snapped off a spray of pale pink hedge roses and presented it to her with a gallant gesture.

Accepting it prettily, she held it to her nostrils and eyed the man beside her thoughtfully.

'Do you enjoy your stay with us?' he asked.

129

'Very much,' she answered warily. 'Lady Kingsclear is kindness itself. And you, Mr Martin, do you like your visit?'

'Why do you ask?'

'Forgive me—but I have come new to all this,' she gestured with her free hand, 'the house and grounds and the countryside. I am a townswoman and the country holds the excitement of the unusual for me ... but you must have seen it many times before. I had imagined that you would care for the entertainments of the town.'

'Oh, I don't know,' he answered vaguely. 'It's dashed difficult to get a ride in town and Grandmama keeps a good stable. There's hunting and shooting in season and enough of my childhood cronies to keep me company.'

They had reached the gates to the drive and, tossing a coin to the tousle-haired boy who came out of the lodge house as they passed, Denvil guided her along the gravel path, talking about the childhood he and Medora and Lyddie had shared.

'How did you cross to the island?' Amy asked mindful of her own wish to pay the isle a visit, as they passed the lake.

'There's a punt somewhere about,' he answered carelessly. 'It's a bit old but I had it out the other day.'

Amy's heartbeat thumped at his words and she decided to search out the boat at the first opportunity that presented itself. She had to curb her impatience that evening, for heavy black clouds had rolled up unnoticed and by the time the ladies were dressing for dinner, huge spots of rain were falling, filling the air with the smell of wet earth. Deciding that the hours after afternoon tea would be the best time for her attempt to land on the island, she waited next day until the house was silent, its inmates busy with their own affairs and uninterested in anything anyone else might be doing, before creeping out of the long windows of the drawing-room, that stood open onto the terrace.

Quickly crossing the smooth grass of the lawn, she was soon standing on the edge of the lake. Delicate willow trees grew down almost to the water, while thick clumps of tall rushes made her task more difficult. Nearly crying with frustration, she was almost on the point of giving up, when she found the punt and wondered why the search had taken her so long; a rope tethering it to the trunk of a tree made its hiding place obvious and only the drooping branches had hidden it from her sight. Lifting her skirt, she scrambled in, untying the rope at the cost of a fingernail and, without more thought, seized a long pole that was lying in the bottom of the boat and pushed out from the side of the lake.

All went well for a while and Amy found the action of poling the punt not unpleasant. A breeze ruffled her hair and the water that dripped from the pole was pleasantly cool as it trickled over her hands. She had left the shallow edge behind and knew by the length of pole that disappeared into the dark water, that she had reached a deeper part of the lake, when with an unexpected snap the pole broke in two, nearly pitching her out of the punt.

Amy stared at the short length of wood left in her hands, before dropping it in the bottom of the punt, she sank down on one of the low seats, while she reviewed her situation.

There appeared to be no current or wind that would carry her to the side and knowing that she would only have to wait until dinner for her absence to be noticed and a search made for her, she decided to wait for rescue with what patience she could muster.

Some time must have elapsed before she realised that her feet were wet. At first she had accepted the dampness that appeared between the boards on which her slippers rested as the general state of boats and had not been unduly interested, but now she viewed the gradually increasing amount of water with growing dismay.

Swimming had never been on the curriculum of the orphanage, the governors having little faith in the fashionable idea that such unnatural activity was beneficial for the health and now Amy knew that she stood no chance of reaching the shore unaided. Raising her voice, she called for help with all her strength

132

but her wailing shout was lost long before it drifted across the lawn and reached the long windows of the Court.

With each passing minute the water gathered momentum, covering her feet and rising remorselessly until it reached the flat board on which she sat. Clutching her wet skirts Amy stood up, the incautious move making the punt move and sway under her. Suddenly it lurched, water gushed over its low sides and then it seemed to melt away from under her and she was thrown into the icy water. Blackness closed over her head and she struck out wildly, arms and legs flailing in panic stricken fright. Abruptly her head broke surface and, gasping for air, she shrieked despairingly, before she sank into the dim depths again.

Something caught her ankle in a vice-like grip and she kicked wildly to free herself, only succeeding in making herself more inextricably a prisoner. A red haze blinding her and with bursting lungs, Amy knew that she could fight no more and with unconscious despair, released the last of her precious air.

As though at a signal, a figure dived on the surfacing bubbles, feeling blindly for her and seized her arm, dragging her free from the retaining weeds with ruthless strength. With senseless panic, the girl clutched at her rescuer, holding him with the strength of fear, threatening to drag them both under the water with her weight, until a hand struck her cheek with enough force to daze her and almost unconscious she was towed to the bank.

Amy opened her eyes to stare at the short blades of grass so near her face. Someone was pummelling her back with hard, painful hands and she murmured a protest, at which she was turned over and wrapped in a coat.

'You really should not go bathing by yourself,' said Ellis, panting from his exertions.

Lying against his chest, Amy gazed at him, taking in the fact that the soldier was minus his coat, very wet and that a strip of green weed was stuck rakishly across one lean cheek.

'Did you...?' she wondered, her voice a sighing whisper.

'Luckily for you I not only happened to be passing on the way to the Court, but am an able swimmer.'

'The pole broke,' she told him, as though that explained all.

'I told her the punt was old,' said someone beyond her vision.

'If you think she can be moved, bring her into the house,' said Lyddie's voice and Amy moved her head wearily to find with surprise that she seemed to be surrounded by most of the inmates of Kingsclear Court.

With very little effort Captain Pensford rose to his feet, Amy clasped against his chest and strode quickly over the grass to the house, followed by a gaggle of excited servants, while

Denvil hovered near offering the aid of his own arms.

Soon Amy was in bed, but not before the sight of her gown wet and stained with green pondweed, had drawn a gasp of horror from her. Following her eyes Lyddie kicked it out of sight and held a cup of hot milk and brandy to her lips.

'Drink this and go to sleep,' she commanded, 'and you'll feel better in the morning,' and stayed beside the other girl until Amy fell asleep.

The sun was streaming in at the open window when Amy awoke and lay for a minute watching the beams of light, while she tried to recall the events of the previous day. At last with a little start of fright she remembered the punt and the water ... and that Ellis Pensford had come to her rescue.

She was prevailed upon to stay in bed for the morning and curled back against the soft pillows, finding that she rather welcomed being treated as an invalid. A nosegay, fresh from the garden was sent up by Denvil and even Medora came to offer the loan of a library book.

Lyddie brought a cup of chocolate and, finding her friend prepared to talk, asked candidly as she sat down on the high bed, 'Whatever happened, Amy? What can have possessed you to take out that old punt?'

'The Three White Ladies,' said Amy. 'Don't you remember what the gipsy said?'

Lyddie stared at her, her mouth open a little. After a while she closed it with a slight snap and cried incredulously, 'The *gipsy*! Oh, Amy, how could you believe such a tarradiddle?'

'I just wondered—I couldn't let it go by without trying—without seeing if there was anything there.' Hunching up against her pillows, her eyes travelled to the window where the lake could be seen and immediately she sat up, craning her neck the better to see. 'What is going on?' she wanted to know. 'There are lots of men—'

Lydia strolled to the window. 'Ellis has some notion ... he and Denvil are down there supervising the estate men who are lifting the punt.'

'But, why?'

'I suppose he thinks it can be repaired,' answered Lyddie casually, returning to the bed. 'You don't know how lucky you are ... if Medora hadn't glanced out of the landing window as we were passing and seen you—'

'I thought it was Ellis who saved me.'

'Indeed it was, but by the time he got you to the bank, he was very pleased to have Denvil's aid.'

'I must offer my thanks to you all,' said Amy soberly and, later that day, after she had made a point of thanking Medora and Denvil, went in search of Ellis, finding him beside the lake, surveying the remains of the punt drawn up on the bank at his feet.

At the sound of her approaching footsteps, he turned and regarded her slowly, his face softening slightly at the sight of her shadowed eyes and the bruise darkening one cheek.

'I ... came to give you my thanks,' she said suddenly shy.

'I am glad to have been of service,' he answered formally and suddenly flung a piece of wood he was holding far out across the water.

'I am sorry to have been a trouble.'

Again he turned to look at her, his mouth unaccountably tight, his dark brows drawn together in a line. 'I would have a word with you,' he said abruptly and, taking her arm, led her across to one of the stone seats that were placed at strategic points in the park.

Standing over her so that she was forced to look up at his tall figure silhouetted against the sky, he seemed not to know what to say. Amy glanced away fingering the fringe edging on her paisley shawl and when at last he spoke, she started nervously.

'What made you take out the punt?'

Amy hung her head and wished he had not asked that particular question; somehow she did not think that Ellis Pensford would have any patience with the gipsy's prophecy. But instead of making the expected scathing remark, he listened to her thoughtfully, swinging his quizzing glass and staring at the water reflectively.

'And so—anyone might have known what the pedlar told you?'

'I suppose so—I made no secret of it.'

'And equally anyone could have guessed that once the meaning of the White Ladies was known to you, you would make an attempt to cross to the island.'

Again she nodded, her eyes puzzled as she looked up at him.

'I very much fear, Miss Clear,' he said softly, 'that someone desires your absence.'

'My—absence?'

'Last night one of the gardeners brought me part of your pole that he had recovered from the lake—both he and I came to the conclusion that it had been partly sawn through ... and when I examined the punt this morning, I discovered that several of the planks appeared to have been deliberately loosened.'

'You mean—' Amy stared at the silken water of the lake and shivered inspite of the warm sun.

'Indeed I do, sweet Coz. It appears to me that the whole episode was engineered from the beginning. It would have been ease itself to bribe the gipsy to mention the island in such a way as to convince you that the solution to your parentage lay there ... After that it only needed for the conversation to be steered in the desired direction—a word here, a hint there. Someone in the Court has given you a very clear warning that if you stay here you will be

138

in danger.'

Huddling in her shawl like a sick bird, Amy hugged herself and shuddered as a sudden thought touched her with icy fingers. Ellis's elongated shadow seemed to hang over her menacingly, as she recalled the two figures dimly seen in the mist a few mornings ago. The gipsy in her red skirt had been unmistakable and the man with her ... might have been a servant, but somehow she didn't think so. He had carried himself with the ease of a gentleman ... and the coat he had worn was well cut and a bright blue ... very like the garment that was covering Captain Pensford's broad shoulders at this very minute.

CHAPTER EIGHT

'Come and sit by me, Amy. I find that I have much to say to you.'

Obediently the girl crossed the paved stones of the terrace and seated herself on the stone seat beside Lady Kingsclear. That lady adjusted the thin shawl about her shoulders, tilted her parasol to shade her face and laid down the novel she had made pretence of reading. Amy looked at her enquiringly and offered to fetch her a glass of lemonade.

'No, no. I have no need for refreshment, child.' The older woman appeared undecided,

139

her cheeks flushed with excitement. 'You must bear with me, Amy,' she said at last. 'Against the advice of a trusted person, I feel that I must speak my mind.'

Again she fell silent, taking the girl's hand and patting it absentmindedly. 'During the weeks you have been with us you may not have been aware that I have watched you closely. I must say that in all that time I have never seen anything in your behaviour but that must please me. In all things you have acted like a gently born lady ... and one that has found a place in my affections.'

'You are very good—' Amy began, but Lady Kingsclear held up her hand and went on.

'I feel sure that you must realise that I have hopes that we may prove to have a near relationship. I wish to say nothing more about that, at the moment, but I know that you must be anxious for your own future and to make certain that whatever happens you may feel settled, I will tell you now, that I intend to make you a legacy in my will. And that there will be a home at the Court for you as long as you wish it.'

Amy murmured her thanks and would have said more, but Lady Kingsclear shook her head firmly and said that she would discuss the matter when her man of affairs had called upon her in answer to a letter she had written.

'You—know I fear to be disillusioned,' she said hesitantly. 'I will hardly allow myself to

140

hope until I am more certain, but I would have you feel secure.' Summoning up a rather watery smile, she presented her cheek. 'Give me a kiss, child,' she said, 'and run along to join your—the other girls. They are cutting roses, just beyond the terrace and doubtless all agog to know what we have been talking about.'

Privately Amy thought that they probably knew only too well; the rose garden was not more than a few paces away from where she and Lady Kingsclear had been sitting and the older woman's voice was high and clear, carrying easily the short distance. However, if Medora had heard she gave no sign of it, merely putting her flower basket into Amy's hands and strolling off declaring that she, for one, was bored with roses and was going to her room.

'I couldn't help but hear,' said her sister as soon as she was out of ear-shot, 'and I am so glad for you. Grandmother has almost recognised you—it couldn't be more obvious that she intends to as soon as she has proof of your parenthood.'

'And—if that proof isn't forthcoming?'

'Then you will live here at the Court. Unrecognised, but favoured—'tis clear that she loves you already.'

'You don't mind?' Amy asked anxiously.

'Never,' she was told stoutly. 'I have longed for a girl cousin all my life. Medora was always satisfied with male company but I have felt a

141

need for a confidante. You and I, Amy, have an affinity.'

Amy happily agreed with her, but even so did not confide her plan for the morrow, feeling that even Lyddie would not agree with what she proposed to do.

By diligent and subtle questioning of the servants, she had discovered that the waggoner's cart passed the gates of the Court that forenoon and that among the places it visited was Alford. Needless to say she was determined to take a place on the cart and, as by great good fortune Lady Kingsclear would be closetted with her lawyer all afternoon, Amy set out stealthily the next day, relying on the hope that Alford was not too far distant and that she would be back before her absence was discovered and she was missed.

Having dressed herself with care in what she considered an appropriate outfit of a plain muslin gown and a drab spencer, she was rather chagrined to find when the carter obligingly stopped and she climbed into the waggon, that her dress stood out among the dark prints and woollen shawls of the country women and farmers' wives. Ignoring the curious glances turned in her direction, she seated herself with all the aplomb she could muster and gave her attention to the slowly passing countryside.

Sometime later, when the hard wooden seat was becoming decidedly uncomfortable and the dust that rose in clouds from the horse's plodding hooves was settling thickly over her clothes and face, she began to doubt the wisdom of her actions, only her utter determination to see the village of Alford making her keep her seat. Trying to ignore the discomforts she settled back, prepared to endure whatever came, when suddenly, with a strident blast on his horn that made Amy glance over her shoulder, a familiar curricle drawn by two grey horses came dashing round a corner of the lane behind them imperiously demanding a clear passage.

The waggoner drew his clumsy cart as much into the side as he could and waited hopefully for the more manoeuvrable vehicle to avoid him, which the curricle did with the greatest of ease, the driver tooling his animals skilfully through the narrow space left him.

Amy ducked her head, relying on the deep brim of her bonnet to hide her face as Captain Pensford passed. A sudden silence and the cessation of movement, made her glance up—to meet the baleful gaze of Ellis's grey eyes as he held his horses and stared across the intervening space at the girl.

The colour flooded her cheeks as she became aware that the other occupants of the wagon had followed his eyes and were regarding her with obvious interest.

'Pray oblige me, Miss Clear,' Ellis said awfully, 'by joining me in my carriage.'

143

Amy shook her head. 'No thank you,' she said politely.

'Do as I say—'

Amy eyed him coolly. 'Don't let me keep you,' she said kindly. 'I believe that heated horses should never be kept standing, though of course, I am sure you know more about such things than I.'

Captain Pensford's eyebrows drew together in an ominous line as his mouth tightened. Tossing the reins to his groom, he climbed down and strode purposefully towards the wagon.

Amy admired the scenery, gazing in rapt attention at the overhead trees and the distant hills . . . anywhere but at the advancing soldier.

'I am waiting, Miss Clear,' he said almost conversationally, 'but I feel that perhaps I should mention that my patience is by no means endless.'

'Best do as he says, miss,' advised the waggoner, 'or we'll be here 'till Doomsday, seeing as I can't get by while that there curricle is blocking the way.'

'This man is trying to abduct me,' Amy said with dignity.

The waggoner eyed Ellis Pensford and then closed one eye in an enormous wink. 'That so, Captain?' he asked. 'I expect it's what comes of mixing with all those Froggies out in foreign places, miss,' he explained to Amy. 'Now you go with him like a good girl . . . and let other folks get about their business.'

Looking round at her fellow travellers, Amy knew by their complacent expressions that there was no help to be had from them and seething with exasperation over her lost expedition, reluctantly stood up.

Ellis was waiting at the end of the wagon and before she could descend, he seized her round the waist and swung her to the ground. For a moment a delicious feeling of helplessness filled Amy, then her feet found the soft, dusty road and she was hurried to the curricle and tossed up into the high seat.

Almost before she had settled her skirts, the tiger sprang up behind, Captain Pensford climbed to his seat beside her and the mettlesome horses plunged forward, encouraged by a ribald shout from the waggoner.

Amy clutched her bonnet, gripping the side of the carriage as the slender vehicle swayed and bounced in an alarming manner high above the road.

'Nervous, Coz?' Ellis asked wickedly, after a quick glance under the deep brim that shaded her pale face.

'Not—at all,' she assured him tartly and untruthfully, her voice tight with anger. 'I can only assume that, with your usual arrogance, you have made sure that this entire stretch of road is free of other traffic.' Turning suddenly on her companion, she eyed him stormily.

145

'How dare you, Captain Pensford, treat me in such a manner? Your cousins may be used to your high-handed actions, but I am not and let me tell you—'

'No, Miss Clear, let me tell you. Neither of my cousins would act in a manner which you seem able to assume very easily. Your behaviour today smacks more of the hoyden adventuress I first thought you, than of a lady of breeding. Good God, woman did no one teach you better than to ride on a common vehicle?'

'You forget that I had not your cousins' advantages,' she cried hotly. 'I would remind you that I was not brought up knowing I was a lady. I am an orphanage miss—as everyone delights in reminding me. I have had to fend for myself all my life and I am quite capable of looking after myself among a few harmless country folk. I am no namby-pamby female who would swoon at the thought of undertaking a journey alone.'

'No—I know you are not.' Something in his quiet reply made her glance quickly up into his face, suspecting that he was laughing at her, but his expression was unwantedly serious as he studied her briefly, before returning his attention to the horses. 'Where were you going?' he asked.

Amy toyed briefly with the idea of refusing to answer, but reluctantly discarded the notion almost at once. 'Alford,' she told him curtly.

'Alford! Have you any idea how long it would take you to get there on that lumbering wagon?'

'I hoped to be back long before dinner.'

'My dear Miss Clear, you would have been lucky to be back before nightfall. What can have persuaded you to undertake such an adventure—have you no care for my aunt's feelings when she finds you not in the house? You, yourself have said how kindly she treats you, even you must know that this is no way to return her goodness. I imagine that you left a note.'

Amy hung her head, playing with the strings of her reticule and watching her gloved fingers through tear-blurred eyes. 'I—believed that there was no need,' she admitted huskily.

'No need! Lady Kingsclear will be worried beyond all measure—' Ellis broke off as a small sound suspiciously like a stifled sob escaped the girl by his side and for a few seconds silence hung between them, before he went on in a more gentle voice. 'Why was this journey to Alford so imperative?'

Amy whisked away a tear with one finger and examined the view on the side away from her companion, hoping that he had not noticed her momentary lapse into feminine emotion. Seeing nothing for it but to make known the whole story, she plunged into her tale and told him the reason behind her escapade in as few words as possible.

147

'I ... see,' Ellis said slowly when she had finished. 'I agree, Miss Clear, Alford would seem a very good place to start your enquiries.'

'It surprises me that no one has thought of it before. The family must have known where Mr Berridge took up his new living after he left Boxdean.'

'Indeed, they must—I can only suppose that at the time the Kingsclears were only too pleased to see him go and that it was forgotten as time went on, until no one recalled it to mind. Even after your arrival made the matter of interest again. I can understand your desire to visit there, Cousin Amy,' he remarked quietly, his strong fingers tightening on the thin reins as, with sudden decision, he drew the horses to a halt.

'John,' he said, addressing the tiger clinging behind, 'do you climb down and make your way back to the Court. Tell Lady Kingsclear that Miss Clear and I are on our way to Alford and have just discovered that Miss Clear forgot to leave a note of explanation. Make our apologies and say all that is proper in the circumstances. She'll think it odd, but do your best to reassure her and say I shall bring my cousin home this evening.'

The groom sprang to the ground with a carefully expressionless face, touched his cap and obediently set off back the way they had so recently travelled.

'Are you always so disregardful of other's

wishes?' Amy wondered, looking over her shoulder at the retreating figure of the tiger.

'John knows more short cuts than I do. He'll be home within the hour,' she was told briefly. 'I thought you were set upon this venture to Alford—and can see no other way of achieving it.'

The girl gazed at him, her eyes wide with speculation. 'Do you really mean to take me?'

'Alford first and *then* the abduction,' Ellis said ironically. 'Did you really find no one to confide in at the Court? Why did you never think to ask Denvil or I to escort you?'

Amy smoothed the fingers of her soft kid gloves. 'After the homily you read me the other day,' she said quietly, 'I thought it best to make no one free of my plans.'

'Very wise,' Ellis said after a perceptible pause. 'Who knows who might take such an opportunity to make away with you—myself included.'

Amy looked at him quickly, almost a shadow of fear in her glance, before seeing the gleam of amusement in his eyes and realising that he was teasing her. 'Oh, la, sir,' she said airily. 'I'm as well able to protect myself as any other well-brought up adventuress.'

The soldier laughed suddenly, white teeth showing briefly in his face, still tanned from the Peninsula sun. 'Let us cry pax for the rest of this journey,' he said, with which suggestion Amy was very willing to agree and so the

149

remaining short distance to Alford was covered in the most amiable way. Ellis proving himself the most interesting of guides to the locality and Amy showing a flattering willingness to listen to his discourse.

Soon they were bowling into the small town and at once ran into difficulties for there were two churches not one as Amy had supposed. However, upon her recalling that the incumbent of Boxdean had mentioned St Paul's in the Fields, all was made plain and, leaving the carriage and pair at the hostelry in the middle of the High Street, Amy and Ellis set out on foot.

Sliding her hand into the arm he offered, Amy was made suddenly aware of the height of her companion and glanced up shyly, not for the first time feeling her own lack of inches.

'We had best hurry,' Ellis commented, glancing up at the heavy grey clouds that were rapidly covering the blue sky. 'I would say that we are in for a rain storm that will set the roads awash—pray Heaven, Miss Clear that we are home before it decides to break.'

The church of St Paul's was on the far side of the town and had obviously once stood alone as its name suggested, but now tiny cottages huddled against its stout stone walls. An aged man climbed out of a grave he was engaged in digging and proclaiming himself the Verger, offered to be their guide, explaining that the vicar was away at a nearby fair, buying himself a steady cob.

Explaining the matter to him, Ellis slid a coin into his gnarled hand and soon they were seated in the vestry with a pile of large books before them.

'Odd, ain't it?' suddenly remarked the old man. 'No one ever wants to see they registers and then, suddenlike, there's folks asking to see them all the time.'

Ellis raised his head. 'Someone else has been here?'

'Another gentleman like your honour was here only the other day.' Watery eyes stared at Captain Pensford, straining across the gloom of the dark vestry. 'Sure it wasn't you sir?' he asked garrulously, eyeing the blue coat and discarded beaver hat. 'He was very like in dress.'

'And so are ten thousand others. Take my word for it, it was not I,' said Ellis easily, but not before Amy's heart had missed a beat as she recalled the fact that Ellis had been away from home a great deal for the last few days. On horse-back and unencumbered the journey to Alford would be easily undertaken, the few hours needed hardly missed and quickly explained.

Suddenly the day seemed to have grown darker, the small, cold room so dim that the grumbling verger reluctantly lit a lamp and left it on the table as he went back to his digging.

Alone with Ellis, Amy sat uneasily in her

151

hard chair, while the soldier seemed deep in thought, his arms folded and his chin sunk into the starched folds of his cravat.

At last he moved, startling her out of her reverie and began searching through the heavy books on the table. 'Ah, here is the one we require,' he said. 'This is the first mention of your Mr Berridge.' Quickly leafing through the musty, closely written pages, he suddenly stopped, read the last date on the left hand page and then the entry at the top of that on the right, before running a finger down the deep crease between.

Amy watched in perplexity, her eyes wide with an unspoken question, as he stood upright again, staring down at her.

'Miss Clear,' he said softly, his voice echoing in the empty church, 'I very much fear that a page is missing.'

'Missing!' Amy stared from him to the book and now, could clearly see the edges, rough and ragged where a page had obviously been removed.

'It would seem to be the pertinent one,' Ellis went on, 'for it is for the year that I would judge your parents to have married—if indeed they were wed ... and now we shall never know. I see that Mr Berridge stops writing a few pages further on and that his death is recorded in a different hand and with the utmost brevity.'

For a moment Amy was crushed by this unexpected blow to all her hopes, but then her usual stubborn optimism returned and she jumped to her feet, facing the man on the other side of the table with her chin high and her eyes sparkling with determination.

'You have mistaken my character, Captain Pensford, if you think that I shall give up so easily. Do you really believe that I would let so puny a thing as a missing page from a Church register deter me? I am determined to prove my parentage.'

Black eyebrows rose and cold grey eyes regarded her from his superior height. 'Miss Clear, you must think me a fool, if you believe that I cannot see that there might very well be another motive behind the removal of the page.' Resting both hands on the open book, he leaned forward, holding her eyes with his. 'Might not your accomplice have taken it—not to hide what was on it, but to make sure that no one would know what was not written there?'

While a few minutes before she had suspected Ellis of being the villain of the piece, she found that she had no liking for being suspected herself and stood up abruptly. 'Take me home, can you please,' she said bleakly and crossed the stone floor without a backward glance, stopping with an exclamation of dismay in the church porch at the sight of torrential rain pouring down.

'Dear me, Miss Clear,' said a voice behind her, sounding amused. 'I believe we will find the roads impassable.'

153

Captain Pensford proved to be a prophet and by the time they reached the inn where the carriage had been left, the main street of Alford was already inches deep in water. Amy clutched her wet and muddied petticoats as she shrugged her arm out of the grip of his strong fingers as he hurried her into the hostelry.

'Could we not have taken shelter?' she demanded.

Ellis smiled down into her damp face and obligingly proffered a large, white handkerchief. 'I thought it best to get here as quickly as possible,' he said mildly. 'My apologies if you are a little wet, Coz, but I am sure the landlady will be only too pleased to dry our clothes for us.'

Quickly rooms were arranged and Amy found herself wrapped in the landlady's shawl while her own dress was removed to the warmth of the kitchen. Staring out of the long window at the drenched street beneath, she watched the stream of water coursing over the rounded cobbles and wondered dismally if she would manage to return to Kingsclear Court that night.

Sometime later, descending the stairs in her dry and newly ironed gown, she found her worst fears justified. Ellis turned from his conversation with the landlord at her entrance and coming forward took her hand to lead her to a table.

'I have it upon the best authority that the

154

roads are quite impassable,' he announced cheerfully, quite disregarding her obvious dismay, 'and have bespoke us rooms for the night and arranged that dinner should be served immediately.'

Hiding her unhappiness, Amy allowed herself to be seated and was silent until the landlord left the small parlour. 'Is there no way we can get back to the Court?' she demanded. 'You must realise that I cannot spend the night here with you—'

'Miss Clear, you disappoint me,' said Ellis blandly. 'For an adventuress you show surprisingly little disregard for convention.'

'You have not even had the forethought to name me your sister,' she added crossly.

'The landlord has known me since childhood. I fear I would have difficulty in explaining away a newly acquired sister.'

Amy glowered at him but was saved from the necessity of finding a suitable reply by the landlord returning at the head of a small procession all of whom carried laiden trays.

The meal was undoubtedly appetising and well cooked but Amy found herself only toying with the food on her plate, uneasily aware of the man opposite watching her with lazy grey eyes ... and of the smallness and intimacy of the private room in which she found herself.

Well aware of the cause of her nervousness, amusement gleamed in Ellis's eyes as he pushed a small plate towards her. 'Try a bonbon,' he

155

advised kindly, 'perhaps they are more to your liking.'

'Is there really no way of getting home tonight?'

'None, Miss Clear. You'd best resign yourself to my company.'

'Captain Pensford—'

Cracking a nut, he glanced across the table at her. 'Miss Clear, whenever you are angry with me, you call me "Captain Pensford" in just such a horrid tone. It's as good a signal as hoisting the Jolly Roger, or crying attack.'

'And when you term me "Miss Clear" I know you are about to be unpleasant,' Amy returned hotly.

'Indeed?' Ellis appeared interested. 'Then for tonight we must use our Christian names and endeavour to keep on the best of terms, if our stay is to be at all pleasant.'

'I, for one, intend to retire early.'

'As you please—but if you do, then so will I and think how your reputation will suffer if anyone should think to question the landlord.'

Amy eyed him closely. 'I thought you had a motive in bringing me here. How lucky it rained, though I suppose it would have been easy enough to arrange some other reason to keep us here.'

'I would have found a wheel cracked or one of the greys would have strained a leg,' he agreed carelessly.

Resting her chin on her hand, she leaned an

156

elbow on the white tablecloth. 'But the reason eludes me,' she confessed. 'I have no cause to imagine that you are wildly enamoured of me.'

Slowly, deliberately, his eyes travelled over her, from the crown of her glossy nut-brown hair, over the flimsy spotted muslin gown to the small kid slippers peeping out from under the hem of her dress. 'You are well enough,' he told her blandly, watching the warm colour touch her cheeks. 'In fact, you are a deal better than I even supposed possible when I first saw you, *then* I thought you a drab little thing.'

Amy raised her thin eyebrows. 'And now, sir?' she asked daringly, her eyes challenging him.

'Now, I find you ... interesting.'

Annoyed with herself for asking the question and refusing to admit that she had half hoped for a compliment, Amy turned her cheek. 'But, you still haven't told me why you brought me here.'

'Let us say rather that you brought yourself. I merely detained you.' He stood up as a maid entered with the tea tray, which she set down on an occasional table near the fire and perforce Amy had to leave the safety of the dining-table and seat herself in front of the ornate teapot. Accepting a cup of tea, Ellis stood looking down at her before seating himself beside her on the high-backed oak settle.

Amy stirred her tea and was annoyed to

discover that her fingers trembled a little. Hastily putting down the betraying spoon, she took an unwary sip of the hot liquid and felt the tears of pain start to her eyes. Glancing at her companion, she found his eyes on her with an enigmatic expression. The unseasonable firelight flickered across his face, touching his hair with tips of flame, while the candles that had been lighted against the dark, wet night outside, did little more than cast shadows.

Unaware of her own apprehensive expression, the girl gazed back at the soldier, unable to remove her eyes from him, or to still the quick beating of the pulse that jumped in her throat. One hand strayed to her mouth as her lips parted a little.

'You seem to specialise in dangerous positions, Miss Clear,' Ellis remarked softly.

'What do you mean?'

Instead of answering, he removed the cup and saucer she still held on her lap and set it down on the table. 'I feel that you cannot have given the matter much thought when you set out on this adventure, Miss Clear. I daresay you believed that you would have only an elderly widow to contend with at Kingsclear Court. Instead of which you find that someone is prepared to eliminate you—witness the escapade at the lake. I feel sure that against such ruthless odds you will be prepared to give up any claim to being the Kingsclear heir.'

Fascinated by the faint, but unmistakable,

air of menace, Amy stared across the narrow space that parted them and shrank back into her corner. Ellis leaned closer, placing one hand on the side of the settle by her shoulder, imprisoning her in the circle of his arm. Rather wildly she looked round suddenly wide-eyed with apprehension.

'I—shall shout,' she warned.

'Do,' he said amiably, 'but I'm afraid it will do you no good. The landlord has had his palm well greased and he will prove strangely and completely deaf to any sounds from this room.'

The colour left Amy's face, leaving her pale and defenceless as she realised with growing alarm the dangers of her position.

Ellis smiled a little, a thin cruel curve to his lips that made Amy wonder that she could ever have thought him kind. 'I think we begin to understand each other,' he remarked gently. 'I believe that we might deal well together, Miss Clear.'

'That I doubt,' she said bravely, the breath catching in her throat, 'but if you tell me what you want, perhaps I can give it my attention.'

'A confession will do with which to start— after that, who knows,' he shrugged deliberately.

'But why? I cannot believe that you envy me my position with Lady Kingsclear.'

'I told you long ago that I had the greatest dislike of being duped—and that extends to include my family. I believe that Lady

Kingsclear is becoming fond of you and I would not have her made unhappy. Rather than that I would help you to remove yourself and make some financial arrangements with you. I stopped believing in ghosts and boggarts ... and lost heirs when I left the schoolroom. Be sure, Miss Clear that you shall not leave this room until I know the truth.'

'And—if I said that all I have ever told you is just that?'

'I would advise you to have a care to your safety—remember the lake, dear Coz, and that whoever wants your absence so much can be relied upon to try again, perhaps with greater success this time.'

Amy stared up at him, moistening her dry lips with the tip of her tongue. 'Do you—are you saying that you are ... the one who—?'

'Afraid, Miss Clear?' he asked and reaching out, touched her cheek with the back of his hand. 'You look like a little mouse bewitched by the kitchen cat and feel as cold as ice.'

'If you have brought me here to murder me, I think it very foolhardy on your part,' said Amy with great resolution, 'and not up to your usual standard of conduct, for not only have you sent a message to Lady Kingsclear by your groom, but I feel that even so complacent a landlord would draw the line at disposing of a dead body.'

A gleam of amusement showed briefly in the cool grey eyes. 'My dear child,' he said. 'If I

160

intended such extreme measures, you may be sure that I would manage it very well … but as it is, all that I require from you would be the confession I have already mentioned. I would rather dispose of you by ridicule and contempt than by murder. I would have my aunt think of you with sorrow at being duped by a trickster, than with anxiety and worry at your disappearance.'

'I have no confession to make—I am … who I am.'

'You have no name,' he said brutally. 'You are a foundling at best and, at worst, a heartless adventuress out to fool an old woman into leaving you her wealth.'

'I don't care about the money—'

'You lie! You are a scheming, lying little cheat, willing to break Lady Kingsclear's heart with your cruel story of being her son's child.'

Amy shook her head. 'I have never said that. I didn't even know she had lost a son until I came here and Jessie told me the tale of Aubrey and the vicar's daughter—'

'Whereupon you made capital out of the old story. Every fact that you have learned about the family history you have used to your advantage. I grant that you have obviously known someone who knew us, but that is easily explained—a servant or even gossip would tell you all you needed to know, before setting out on such an adventure. Even the missing page from the register is easily explained away with the aid of an accomplice.'

'No—no!' Amy pushed at the arm that imprisoned her, then struck out at the face so near her own. Before she could hit him, her wrist was caught and held and as her other hand flew at his eyes, that too was seized and held against his chest.

'Let me go, oh, let me go!' she cried, struggling in vain as his grip tightened.

His face impassive, he let her feel his strength, until with a little gasp, she stopped fighting and, turning her head away, bit her trembling lip to stifle a sob.

Changing his grasp to hold her wrists with one hand, he slid his free hand behind her shoulders and slowly drew her against him. Amy saw the grey glitter of his eyes before his mouth closed over hers with brutal force.

When at last he raised his head, Amy was breathless and trembling as she hid her face from his searching look. With ruthless fingers, he turned her chin up, taking in her flushed cheeks and the frightened hurt behind the tears sparkling on her lashes.

Suddenly releasing her, he abruptly stood up and crossing to the fire, stood with his hands on the mantelshelf, staring down into the flames. As suddenly turning back into the room, he returned to the settle and seated himself beside her again.

Trying to hide her alarm, Amy refused to meet his glance, staring woodenly ahead, only too aware of his nearness. 'I had supposed soldiers to be men of honour,' she said bitterly, 'but I see I was mistaken. If I had a kinsman to defend me, or even a name to call my own, I doubt that you would have treated me so.'

Possessing himself of her shaking hands that were straining together in her lap, he gently turned her towards him, but hanging her head, she avoided his eyes, leaving only the top of her dishevelled hair to meet his gaze.

'My apologies—I can only ask for your forgiveness, Amy.'

Against her will the girl raised her startled face, catching her breath in surprise.

'I had to find out if you were the innocent girl you appeared to be—or the trickster which I believed you.'

'You kissed me just to find out?' she demanded indignantly.

'Partly—' Ellis's mouth curved with amusement, 'but I won't deny that it is something which I have long desired to do.'

Snatching her hands away, Amy tried to hide her mortification as anger swiftly superseded the fear she had felt. 'And have you decided?' she asked in a high, clear voice, 'Whether I am an adventuress or not?'

'Unless you are better talented than Mrs Siddons herself, I'd wager my fortune that you are—who you are.'

Well aware of the ambiguity behind his words, Amy raised her eyebrows. 'And that

163

is—a girl from an orphanage, who might, or might not, be an heiress.'

'Indeed.'

'Not only that, but after spending the night here alone with you, in the eyes of the world I am ruined—'

'And still in danger of your life.'

Amy looked at him, while a little pulse beat in the base of her neck. 'I wish I had never met you,' she said clearly.

Ellis gave a short laugh. 'That, I can well believe. However, I think I have it within my power not only to make amends, but to keep you safe as well.'

Amy was curious. 'How so?' she asked politely.

'Marry me, cousin,' he answered lightly.

The candles danced a wild jig round her head, while the shadows leaped and swayed like mad things, then the world settled back into place and she could see the man beside her clearly again. For a moment she wondered at his cool effrontery, before she seized the chance to pay back some of the insults she had received during the last few hours.

'Have you run mad?' she cried. 'I'd rather be a governess!'

After an almost imperceptible pause, Ellis stood up and bowed. 'As you will,' he said indifferently, looking down at her. 'Let me ring for the maid to escort you to your chamber— after the exertion of the day, you will wish to

164

retire early.'

There was an uncomfortable silence until the maid came, at least on Amy's part, but Captain Pensford retired to the window embrasure and stared out at the wet street, seeming to have lost all interest in his companion.

Once in the security of her chamber, Amy sank down on the bed and indulged in the tears that she had so far suppressed, allowing herself to ponder on the reason behind Ellis's astounding proposal and her own abrupt refusal, facing the fact that pique had lost her the chance of being chatelaine to a rich country seat ... and against her will, wondering what being wife to the autocratic Ellis Pensford would have been like. Involuntarily, her fingers touched her bruised lips where his kiss seemed still to linger and reluctantly she was forced to admit to herself that there was something she would much rather be than either a governess ... or even heir to the wealth of the Kingsclears.

CHAPTER NINE

Lady Kingsclear seemed to accept her nephew's excuses with equilibrium, her mind being much taken up with the visit of her man of affairs, Mr Grey, the previous day and the forthcoming dinner she was giving to formally introduce Amy to society. Having read her a mild scold, she dismissed her and turned back to her correspondence, while the girl wandered somewhat disconsolately away.

Medora was paying a visit to some friends and even Lyddie was little interested in Amy's adventures, having been struck by violent toothache the night before. 'I should have visited the dentist long ago,' she moaned, holding her swollen cheek. 'Jessie has stuffed it with a clove and dosed me with laudanum, but nothing eases it.' She suddenly turned to the other girl and clutched her arm. 'Will you come with me? We could go quickly to see Mr Peak in Leahook, before my courage evaporates.'

'Of course,' Amy answered instantly, 'but we should have a man with us. Shall I ask Denvil?'

'I'd liefer have Ellis—he is one to depend upon and has such a comforting shoulder.'

Amy perceived that Lydia held quite a different view of the soldier to her own, but only offered to send a message.

'No—for then we shall have to wait and really I feel that I can wait no longer. Do you ask Denvil.'

Amy pressed her back in a chair. 'Lie still,' she counselled, 'while I arrange everything,' and soon they were seated in the depths of the cumbersome family coach, the sufferer well wrapped against chills, while the inestimable Jessie hovered with smelling salts ready to hand and Denvil gave them the comfort of his manly presence.

A groom having ridden ahead, Mr Peak was waiting for his patient when they arrived. An examination showed that the only treatment possible was removal of the offending tooth, which was speedily accomplished to the relief of all concerned and within half an hour of descending from the coach, Lyddie was being helped into it again.

Jessie proceeded to wrap her in blankets and Amy waited in the road until the task was completed, Denvil at her elbow. Idly gazing about the empty main road of the little country town, her attention was attracted by the odd behaviour of a small boy, gradually creeping nearer. Suddenly darting forward, he seemed to fall against her companion, who turned with a smothered oath and, with surprising speed, seized the child before he could run away.

'Take my purse, would you?' he cried, dealing him a stinging clout about the head. 'It's the Beadle for you, my lad.'

'Oh, no!' Amy protested. 'I'm sure he meant no harm. How do you know he is a thief?'

For answer Denvil pulled the boy's hand out of the pocket of his ragged breeches and forced it open to reveal a small silk purse lying in the grubby palm. 'He's a pick-pocket—a villain and the sooner he's transported the better,' he told her and shook his captive, who promptly burst into tears, rubbing his eyes with dirty

167

fingers, while one bare foot twisted about the other.

'I—was 'ungry,' he cried between sobs, trying vainly to escape from the strong fingers that gripped his bony shoulders.

Amy fell on her knees in the dusty road and captured both the child's hands, dragging them away from his face. 'Don't cry,' she said. 'No one will hurt you,' and as the boy grew quieter, she wiped his dirty face with her handkerchief. 'Why did you take the purse?'

Denvil made an impatient gesture. 'Because he's a young thief and as such should be locked away where he can't harm decent people.'

The girl glanced up. 'Don't you see he's half starved?' she asked. 'And almost frightened to death—now do be quiet while I talk to him.' Pushing the shock of thick hair out of his eyes, she turned back to the boy. 'Now, tell me your name and where you come from.'

'Jem, miss.'

'Jem—that's a nice name. Jem, who?'

'Don't know, miss.' The boy squirmed and tried to wipe his nose against his shoulder. 'And I don't know neither where I come from.' In a sudden rush of confidence, he went on, 'I was ole Green's sweepboy, see and I climbed chimneys. That's my trade, miss, but I growed too much. I'm too big to get up the passages now and ole Green he turned me off.'

'What? Left you to wander and make your own living?' Amy was indignant. 'I've never heard of such a thing.'

'Good Lord, Cousin Amy,' put in Denvil, 'the boy's seven or eight ... old enough to fend for himself without resorting to theft.'

'Old enough! Pray tell me, sir, what you were doing at such a great age? I suppose you were a master of tree-climbing or telling your lessons and eating the meals that came to your schoolroom each day and had, I daresay, no more idea of fending for yourself than this baby has.'

'I am sure that your womanly spirit is all compassion, but under the circumstances, you must allow me to be the better judge,' Denvil told her rather stiffly. 'A thief must be punished, and Lyddie will be wondering at the delay. If you will climb into the coach, I will make the necessary arrangements for the boy and you need not concern yourself in the matter.'

'But I *am* concerned. Do you think I could sleep easy in my bed, if I let you take this child to the Beadle?' Amy's hold tightened on the boy's hands and aware of the half understood discussion going on above his head, Jem gave a frightened wail and opened his mouth to make the world aware of his woes.

Amy's brow wrinkled with anxiety as Jessie put her head out of the coach window and demanded to know what was amiss. Denvil picked up the boy bodily and tried to bear him off, while Jem's thin fingers fastened into the

169

sleeve of Amy's jacket with the determination of fear. It was at that moment that a curricle bowled along the road and, seeing the disturbance ahead, the driver pulled in behind the coach and lazily surveyed the scene.

'Pray put that unfortunate child down, before you tear him in half,' Ellis advised, with amusement in his calm voice and Amy turned to him in relief.

'How glad I am to see you,' she said sincerely, in her anxiety not noticing the sudden intentness of his gaze as he looked down at her from his perch over the matching horses. 'Denvil wants to hand this little boy over to the Beadle and only because he tried to take his purse.'

'The young scoundrel's a thief,' put in Denvil, somewhat sullenly, aware that he was losing the battle, but unable to understand the reason behind his defeat.

The grey eyes were turned back to Amy and one mobile eyebrow rose into a peak. 'And what say you, cousin?'

Unaware of the picture she presented, her face framed in the silk of her bonnet, her dark eyes wide with supplication as she looked up at him, Amy raised one hand in a small pleading gesture. 'He's ... such a little one,' she said, 'and was hungry. He'd been turned off by his master, you see.'

Ellis made an imperious gesture. 'Come here, boy,' he said and the culprit recognising

170

the authority behind his voice, edged unwillingly forward as Denvil reluctantly released his hold on him. 'Have you told this lady the truth?' the soldier asked.

'Yes, Guv'nor. Cross me 'eart. Green was a master sweep and I was 'is boy—until I growed.' With sudden inspiration he dragged up his sleeves and trousers to show his bony knees and elbows. 'There's me scars where they pickled me to stop me rubbing raw against the chimney walls.'

For a moment they all gazed at the marks he displayed with obvious pride, before Amy turned abruptly away, tears pricking her eyes.

'I—didn't know,' Denvil said in a shocked voice. 'Do they really do that to them?'

'And light fires under us,' Jem added with relish. 'Cor, that don't half make us run.'

Amy swung back to Ellis as he climbed down and touched his arm. 'Please—do something. Could I pay for him to be apprenticed to a decent man?'

The soldier took both her hands into a comforting grip. 'Have you the money?' he asked and smiled as her downcast head told the truth. 'Never mind. I have an idea that might help.' Holding out a hand to the boy, he waited impassively as the child came slowly towards him. Turning up the tousled head, he studied the thin face below, taking in the clear blue eyes and the impish curve to the wide mouth between the tear-stained cheeks. 'Well, Jem, it

171

just happens that I am looking for a stable boy. Would you like to come and work for me?'

Jem's eyes travelled over the resplendent blue coat of the man that held him, taking in the vision of shining horseflesh and dashing curricle behind and a grin of pure joy flashed out on his pale face. 'Work for a bang up, swell cove like you. Wouldn't I *just*,' he cried with enthusiasm and his bare feet danced a jig for happiness in the dust.

Amy sighed with relief. 'Oh—thank you,' she said softly. 'You don't know how grateful I am.'

Ellis looked down at her for a long minute. 'Gratitude is a poor thing,' he answered for her ears alone before, slipping a hand under her elbow, he assisted her into the waiting coach.

She caught a last glimpse of Jem being thrown up into the curricle as they drove off and it occurred to her how easy their first meeting after the scene at Alford had been, before she settled back in her seat prepared to explain to Lyddie what had happened.

'Truly, I had no idea,' said Denvil, when she had finished her tale. 'I didn't know that such things were possible.'

'How else could these great chimneys be swept?' asked Jessie practically. 'They're too wide and twisting for any brush to clean—of course a climbing boy has to do it. You gentry just don't think about things like that.'

Denvil had the grace to look ashamed at her

172

words and taking pity on him, Amy changed the subject, talking about the forthcoming dinner party with such enthusiasm that even Lyddie roused herself enough to show a little interest. 'I shall have a new gown,' she announced from her corner, stirring among the rugs and shawls that covered her. 'Amy—I believe that I shall feel well enough this afternoon to look at the fashion-plates in Grandmama's copies of the *Ladies Magazine*. We could both choose a style and ask Mrs Mulchett to make them up for us.'

A few days later, when Lyddie's toothache was a thing of the past, the ladies set out for Leahook with the firm purpose of arranging with the mantua-maker that she should undertake the sewing of two dinner gowns. Mrs Mulchett professed herself delighted at the prospect and at once set about displaying bolts of material and selections of lace and ribbon.

With the memory of Medora's remarks about the white gown selected for her by Lady Kingsclear, this time Amy was determined to choose her own gown and firmly declined the pale pinks and blues presented to her.

'I see a roll of stuff on the shelf that interests me,' she said and knew at once, when the material was spread out for her appraisal that she had found the very thing for which she was looking.

'The very best oyster satin, Miss,' Mrs

173

Mulchett assured her, smoothing the shining folds of pale almond green with loving fingers. Glancing at her client's nut-brown hair, she nodded approvingly. 'Not everyone could wear it, but with your colouring—'

'How clever you are, Amy,' said Lyddie admiringly. 'I wish there was something that went with this horrid hair of mine—but what goes with ginger? I suppose I shall have to have blue again. You have no idea how tired I am of pale blue. I seem to have worn it since my school days.'

Amy looked at her friend consideringly. 'I think your hair is very pretty,' she said. 'Think how we all envy you your curls when we have to wind up our hair each night with curlpapers. 'Tis a pity that pale colours are the fashion, for I believe that darker shades would show off its colour better.'

'Heavens! I've always tried to subdue it.'

'Have you ever worn another shade of blue—there's a lovely turquoise there.' Amy pointed and at once the dress-maker produced a length of blue-green crepe, which she draped expertly over the other girl's shoulder, exclaiming with ready admiration as she did so.

'Have I not suggested such a shade before, miss, but you were so struck on blue—which of course is a very becoming colour, but this, now, is the very latest thing. It's all these antiquities from Egypt, you know. I can assure you that

174

no one in the district has had the courage to buy a length yet.'

'It's pretty,' sighed Lyddie, holding the material against her as she admired her reflection in the mirror on the wall. 'It makes my wretched hair quite a reasonable colour. Silver ribbons, Mrs Mulchett, if you please— but I'll leave the rest to you. You know what I like.'

The dress-maker smiled and turned to Amy. 'And you, Miss Clear?' she cooed. 'What trimmings would you like?'

'I am sure, that with tucks on the bodice and a half train at the back, you would advise me to have matching ribbons,' Amy said diplomatically, having already noted Mrs Mulchett's penchant for adding trimmings to the original design.

'Miss doesn't think it a little severe?' the older woman asked, eyeing the simple, elegant dress shown on the fashionplate. 'Well— perhaps with jewellery and flowers...'

'You can always be relied upon for good taste,' Amy told her and avoided Lyddie's twinkling eyes, while the final arrangements were made.

'Are you always so good at getting what you want?' the other girl asked when they were seated once more in the coach, being driven back to the Court. 'I vow you twisted Madam Mulchett round your finger. I like "trimmings" as she calls them, but I know you don't.' She

175

hesitated a little awkwardly, before asking, 'Forgive me—but is it because of what Medora said about your white ball gown?' As Amy looked away, she went on impulsively. 'Because if so, there really is no need. She only said it to worry you. Medora has always to be the first—the *best* in everything and when she saw you looking so different and delightful, she was a little jealous.'

Amy looked at her incredulously. 'Of me!'

'Of you.' Lyddie smiled at her. 'I truly believe that you have no idea of what an attractive creature you are. Not precisely in the ordinary way, perhaps, but I happen to know that you have made a great hit with the gentlemen. We will probably stand up for a few dances after Grandmama's dinner party and I am sure that you will be in great demand.'

It was with Lydia's words ringing in her ears that Amy surveyed herself in the mirror some days later. Reddish hair gleamed in the candle light, while sparkling dark eyes emphasised her smooth creamy skin above the pale green dress. One glance told her how right she had been to choose that precise, unusual shade and, well pleased with herself, she turned away drawing on her long kid gloves.

Lydia was a vision in her turquoise gown, reminding Amy of one of the ancient goddesses, while for once Medora found herself almost outshone in a dress of the palest pink gauze.

'My beautiful girls,' exclaimed Lady Kingsclear fondly when they went to show themselves to her and blinked away an emotional tear. 'How proud your Grandpapa would have been.'

Wilkins brought up posies for the ladies that had been sent with Captain Pensford's compliments. An oppulent bouquet of red roses for Lady Kingsclear, a pink nosegay for Medora, a spray of golden flowers for Lyddie and a single white camellia for Amy.

'Only one flower,' Medora commented disparagingly, but Amy felt that the soldier had shown surprising insight into her own preferences by his choice and with great daring, pinned it not onto her dress, but tucked the stem into the curls on the top of her head.

'Very becoming,' approved Lady Kingsclear, a twinkle in her eyes, 'though hardly conventional.'

'Shall I remove it?'

'Indeed, no. The great thing in the fashionable world is to know when convention may be flouted. I believe you have that gift, child.'

When the ladies descended the stairs, Denvil and Ellis were waiting in the hall looking very formal in their black evening dress and by the way his eyes lingered on her hair, Amy knew that Ellis had noticed the use to which she had put his flower. However the initial awkward moment was smoothed over by his talking easily about Jem and soon she was able to forget her momentary nervousness and join in the light conversation, until the guests arrived and the gentlemen offered their arms to the ladies, prior to entering the big dining-room.

Amy found herself seated next to Ellis, but by convention was forced into conversation with the gentleman on her left. Lady Kingsclear's cook had surpassed herself with the magnificence of the meal provided and the lady at the head of the table graciously accepted many compliments on the other's behalf. At last the signal was given and the ladies rose to leave the men to their port, while they retired to the trays of tea waiting in the with-drawing room.

Soon the gentlemen rejoined them and Medora was persuaded to entertain them upon the pianoforte. Amy was aware that Denvil made many attempts to join her, but she was surrounded by a group of the local young men and it was not until later that evening that he found her momentarily alone. She felt herself grow a little warm under the obvious admiration in his glance as he bent over her hand.

'Will you dance, cousin?' he asked, holding her hand a little longer than was necessary.

'I am a little tired,' she admitted ruefully.

'Then let me find you a seat and a glass of lemonade,' he suggested and before she could protest, lifted the heavy curtain covering one of the deep window embrasures to reveal the wide window-seat. 'Cool—and private,' he pointed out with a smile and after seeing her seated, left to find the promised refreshment.

Amy listened to the music from the hall as the musicians struggled to provide the dances called for by the younger guests. Within a short time Denvil was back with a glass of cool liquid and taking the fan that hung from a loop round her wrist, he fanned her while she sipped.

'I have no need to ask if you are enjoying yourself, for 'tis easy to see that you are.' Leaning back, he gazed at her until she raised her eyebrows inquiringly. 'I'll confess that you surprise me, Cousin Amy. The other day you were prepared to fight for that little ragamuffin—kneeling in the street without a care for your gown and today . . . you appear so poised and elegant that one would suppose that you had no knowledge of the lower classes.'

'You forget that I come from an orphanage,' Amy reminded him quietly. 'I am not so used to having things done for me that I am unaware of the people who do them.'

'We—*I* am not so uncaring as you think. Today I asked Ellis if I could take the boy, Jem. He seemed to think that it would be unwise to unsettle the child again and of course, with an establishment of his own, Ellis finds such things easier to arrange.'

Amy turned to him, her eyes shining. 'How

179

kind of you, Denvil,' she said, pleased by his action and at once found her hands clasped in his.

'Amy—you must be aware of my feelings, however well I have fought to hide them,' he declared to her surprise. 'For weeks I have laboured to conceal the emotions I have felt—'

Amazed, Amy struggled to free her hands, saying with some asperity, 'What emotions, sir? You have hidden them so well that I have not the least notion of what you mean.'

'Ah, I see I have been too quick for you—and who can blame a young female for desiring a long courtship, but my heart would speak even though my brain told me to bide my time until you were ready to hear my declaration. Miss Clear—Amy, you must know that I have long held you in the deepest admiration. Your presence here at the Court has filled what would have been an empty sojourn with delight. Have you not wondered at my continued stay, when I only intended a short visit?'

'Your grandmother—your cousins,' murmured the girl a little confused, as she recalled mention of his debts that Lyddie said kept Denvil in the country to avoid dunning by various tradesmen.

'You—only you, my dearest Amy,' she was told fervently and the man beside her carried her fingers to his lips again, while his eyes watched her above her hand.

180

Glancing round the enclosed space almost like a room, Amy became aware of her indiscretion in allowing herself to be taken into the alcove by Denvil Martin and snatched her hand away, saying indignantly, 'You go too far, Mr Martin. Pray escort me back to the others.'

As she would have risen, Denvil put out a detaining hand. 'Mistake me not, cousin,' he said earnestly, 'even though our positions are not equal, my proposal is of the most honourable.'

Amy drew herself up to her full height. At first she had been amazed, then puzzled and now she felt the full force of her anger as she flashed him a look of withering scorn. 'So I had supposed,' she said, her voice shaking with rage.

A moment longer he held her hand, seeming unaware of the emotions he had aroused in her. 'Won't you think about it?' he asked. 'I know my grandmother would look upon the match with approval ... and would doubtless settle something upon us. As my wife you would have position and security, both of which, you'll forgive me mentioning the fact, you so far lack.'

For once lost for words, Amy wrapped him smartly across the knuckles with her ivory fan, twitched herself free as his grip involuntarily slackened and pushing aside the curtain without regard for discretion, marched out of her place of concealment ... and straight into the arms of the gentleman who happened to be passing.

Expertly steadying her, Ellis took in the spots of high colour on her cheek bones and at once put himself between her and any guests who might notice her obvious distress.

'What has happened to put you in such a passion?' he asked, his eyes going above her head to the curtain falling into place across the alcove she had left so precipitously.

'I am not in a passion,' Amy spat. 'I cannot imagine what can have given you such an odd notion.' Blinking back the tears of rage that threatened to overflow and spill down her cheeks, she struggled to control her emotions. 'Pray let me go—I wish to go to my room ... a tear in my dress ... '

Without a word the soldier hurried her out into the terrace, which fortunately happened to be empty, seated her upon one of the stone seats, dropped a large handkerchief into her lap and turned away until she had effected repairs to her wet countenance.

'I am better now,' she said in a small voice and he turned back to her, matching the dark night in his black and white evening clothes. Although the moon was hidden behind clouds, the diamonds in his shirt front twinkled like small stars and, half hidden by shadows, his angular face took on the air of Mephistopheles as he towered over her.

'Did someone try to take advantage?' he asked abruptly. 'You have no need to cry, they shall answer to me for their impertinence.'

'No—no!' Amy put out a hand in an imploring gesture. 'Nothing of the kind—I would not trouble you.'

Her hand was taken in a warm grasp and Amy felt strangely comforted as he sat beside her. 'Was it one of those young bloods that have been paying court to you all evening? They are easily dealt with, I assure you. Just tell me his name and I'll bring him to you with an apology on his lips.'

'I would liefer far that it was forgot,' she told him. 'And indeed it was partly my own fault for allowing myself to take the seat behind the curtain.'

'That I'll allow,' Ellis agreed, 'but I would have thought you held more intelligence than to accept such an invitation from one of our local gentry—' Suddenly a thunder-struck expression crossed his face. 'It must have been one of your acquaintances—by God, it was Denvil!'

A finger beneath her chin relentlessly turned up her face when she would have avoided his eyes. 'Well, Miss Clear—*was* it my cousin who made this improper advance?'

'It was hardly improper, sir—he asked me to marry him.'

For a moment his hold on her chin tightened and he was very still as a frown gathered on his

183

forehead. 'Did he, by Jove,' he said softly to himself before turning a considering gaze back to the girl. 'And why did that put you in such a pother, I wonder?'

Amy pushed his hand away and this time he let her go. 'I—hardly know,' she confessed. 'It seemed unreal, like someone play-acting. He seemed to think that I should be grateful that he was proposing marriage ... and, and not something quite different.'

'I can imagine that it would have annoyed you,' Ellis said gravely and Amy looked up quickly, but could find no sign of amusement in his expression. 'May I ask, Coz, what reply you gave him?'

She hung her head, struck by the enormity of her conduct. 'I ... hit him with my fan,' she admitted unhappily.

The soldier shook with silent laughter. 'Oh, Amy,' he said, 'at least I was spared that—and I had taken a kiss as well as making an honourable proposal!' Suddenly growing sober, he took her hands again and constrained her to face him so that the light streaming from the open windows behind them fell full upon her face. 'I—think you were not altogether wise. Has no one told you that a gentleman has quite as much pride as a lady?' He rubbed the backs of her hands with his thumbs as he went on. 'Don't look so downcast, Coz ... but take my advice to seek out Denvil and leave him with a little hope. I am sure you can manage it tactfully.'

'I daresay—but I am not at all sure that I want to,' rejoined the girl, thoughtfully. 'I felt he was more interested in any annuity Lady Kingsclear might provide than in actually gaining me for a bride.'

'Make allowances for a man making a proposal that he was not at all sure was welcome ... Every man must know embarrassment under such circumstances and perhaps, Denvil wasn't good at putting his feelings into words. After all what other reason could there be behind his actions?'

Amy's expression cleared. 'You are right,' she said. 'I am afraid I acted foolishly ... you must forgive me.'

'Blame the weather,' Ellis smiled. 'A storm has been brewing all evening. The air is oppressive and still, quite enough to make us all uneasy and edgy.'

'I'll say all that is right and proper when I see him,' she promised, but her good intentions were foiled by something beyond her control, for at that moment the storm broke, as a dazzling white streak of light flashed across the sky, followed by a crashing clap of thunder.

Ellis hurried her inside and for a while the braver guests watched the lightning playing about the park, while the more timid souls drew the curtains and prayed for deliverance. At last a few drops of rain fell and as the noise ceased the guests seized the opportunity to call for their carriages and make their way home before the storm returned with renewed violence. As a strong wind blew up, lashing at the trees that surrounded the house, the thunder and lightning returned, dancing wildly across the open lawns, dimming the candles and making the rooms as light as day with its vigour. Ellis allowed himself to be persuaded to stay the night by an obviously nervous Lady Kingsclear and a servant was sent to fetch his night things from Raven Hall.

His aunt insisted upon all the curtains being drawn over the windows of the house and every mirror being covered, before allowing herself to be led away to bed by a sympathetic Jessie. The young ladies retired to their own chambers and before long the house grew quiet as its inmates slept, albeit a little uneasily as the now distant storm rolled around the surrounding hills.

Exactly what wakened her Amy never knew, but suddenly she was sitting up in bed, her ears straining for the sound that had disturbed her. She was just beginning to relax again against her pillow, when a piercing shriek filled the air with alarm, bringing her to her feet, the terrible sounds still ringing in her brain.

Snatching a wrap from the foot of her bed, she ran from the room, stumbling over something that lay just outside and entangled her feet in its soft folds. Other doors were opening now and voices could be heard raised in query and without conscious thought, Amy picked it up and ran on in the direction she judged the screams to have come. For a second a faint, elusive perfume seemed to fill the passage and then it was gone.

Arriving at Lady Kingsclear's chamber, she found the door open onto the corridor and Ellis already comforting his aunt, who lay back against her pillows, her lace cap awry and her frightened face holding a slight tinge of grey.

Before Amy could see more, others arrived and the maid, Jessie pushed her way through to her mistress. Under her instructions, Denvil held a burnt feather to his grandmother's nose, while she chaffed her hands. Soon the colour returned to the pale face and after a while faded blue eyes were opened and gazed about at first blankly and then with returning alarm.

'The White Nun!' she quavered, her shaking hand pointing to the door. 'I saw her standing there—looking at me—'

'Now, Aunt Charlie,' soothed Ellis, bending over her. 'You've had a bad dream—you know how storms always upset you.'

Wildly she clutched at his hands. 'No—no! I was awake ... and saw her quite clearly, with two huge black eyes staring at me. I was so frightened that I closed my eyes ... and called out—and when I looked again she had gone.'

One plump hand held her chest as she breathed quickly and gazed up at her tall nephew. 'Ellis—you know what she is

187

supposed to mean?' she half whispered.

'Dear Grandmama, you have many years before you,' put in Denvil, not as tactfully as he might and, as all the occupants of the room turned their eyes upon him, he coloured a little, aware of his mistake and stumbled into an explanation. 'We all know what a visit from the Nun is supposed to mean. I was only trying to comfort Lady Kingsclear.'

'I vow I knew something was in the air,' declared Medora suddenly. 'Such a night as this would serve to stir the spirits and make their shades walk abroad. Does no one else feel a ... chill in the room?'

Lady Kingsclear moaned faintly and Ellis turned an impatient glance on his cousin. 'An you have nothing of more use than such idiotic remarks, my dear Medora, I would suggest that you take yourself back to your bedchamber,' he remarked with asperity.

She bridled a little at his tone and tossed her blonde curls. 'I shall stay with Lyddie,' she said. 'I am too much of a fright to sleep alone after this.'

His grandmother caught again at Ellis's hand, clearly uneasy at the thought of being left alone and Amy stepped diffidently forward.

'Would you like me to stay with you?' she offered a little hesitantly. 'If there is no one else you'd prefer, of course ... I don't mean to usurp anyone's place, but I thought ... if

188

Lyddie and Medora...' Slowly her voice trailed away as she became aware that everyone was staring at her. 'I don't mean to put myself forward...' again her voice faltered and, following their concerted gazes, she glanced down at what she held.

'What have you there?' demanded Medora, suspiciously and, darting forward, she dragged it out of the other girl's hands to look at it in bewilderment. 'A—sheet!' she said in a blank voice and spread it against her skirt.

As she held it out for them all to see, two black smears of soot made a travesty of a face against the white material and after a second of shocked silence, she sucked in her breath quickly as she took in the significance of what she held.

'It was you!' she hissed at Amy. 'You did it. You tried to frighten Grandmama. You wicked, wicked creature.' Her voice was high anger.

'Now, wait a while,' adjourned Denvil. 'I daresay Amy found it somewhere and brought it along by accident.'

'Yes, that's just what happened,' Amy told them and drew back before the scorn in their eyes, realising how unconvincing her words sounded coming after what Denvil had said. 'Oh, why won't you believe me?' she cried and turned imploringly to Lyddie, who so far had said nothing. '*You* believe me, don't you?'

'I—of course,' answered the other girl, but

189

her momentary hesitation had been enough for Amy.

'Where did you find it?' came Ellis's quiet tone and slowly Amy looked up to find him standing in front of her, like a bulwark between her and the rest of the room.

'What's the use?' she asked dispiritedly.

'I would like to hear your story.'

'It's not a story,' she flashed. 'It was on the floor in the doorway of my room—'

'What an odd place for the ghost to shed her skin,' remarked Medora scornfully. 'I wonder that you don't make up a better tale than that.'

'And you saw no one?' went on Ellis, his voice rising above hers.

Amy shook her head, 'But I—think I might have heard someone earlier, before Lady Kingsclear called out.'

'You interest me, cousin,' observed Ellis and turned away to stand by the fireplace, the long skirts of his brocade dressing-gown swinging about his feet. 'Now, let us see if anyone will confess to having been abroad at such a time.' His eyes wandered over the assembled household. 'As long as your journey was legitimate be assured that no harm will come to you,' he said and waited impassively for an answer to his query. After a while he stirred and sighed. 'No? Then we can only conclude that the wanderer must have been the wearer of this,' he touched the sheet that Medora had dropped, with a contemptuous toe.

'It must have been intended as a joke,' burst out Lyddie. 'No one would play such a trick, meaning deliberately to frighten Grandmama. I cannot believe that anyone would be so cruel. Whoever it was must, surely, have mistaken her room in the darkness ... and the passages are dark, for all the curtains are closed, remember.'

'Your unwillingness to see any bad does you credit, but in this case, I believe that the choice of victim was quite deliberate.'

'Surely, 'tis best forgotten,' said Denvil. 'After all it has never happened before...' His voice trailed away and he glanced uncomfortably across at Amy. 'Not that I infer anything by those facts, of course,' he said.

''Tis strange, surely,' put in Medora maliciously, 'that so many unusual happenings have occurred this summer ... since Miss Clear left her orphanage, in fact.'

'You are unkind,' Lyddie said quietly, but her voice lacked conviction and her eyes slid away from Amy as she nervously tied and retied the sash at her waist.

'I think it is time I had a say in the matter,' Lady Kingsclear said from her bed, where she had been watching the proceedings. 'As one most nearly involved and as head of this household, I would have the last word.' Her voice shook slightly and the plump fingers tugging at the lace on her sheets betrayed how hard it was for her to keep her emotions under control. 'Amy—come here.'

Almost reluctantly the girl moved and slowly drew near the high bed. Anxiously her eyes examined the ravaged face under the lace cap, but what she saw gave her no comfort. 'You—don't believe it was I?' she whispered.

'When I received your letter,' began Lady Kingsclear, staring down at her trembling hands, 'I sent for you, for no good reason, save that I was in need of diversion, but when I saw you ... I felt a faint hope that you might be my lost grandchild. Despite good advice and all the evidence to the contrary, I persisted in my belief ... because I had grown fond of you and hoped ... that my affections were returned.'

For the first time she looked at the girl standing beside the bed. 'Love must be returned for it to have something to be nurtured on ... The thought that you could have done this thing to me is quite insupportable. I find that I can no longer bear your presence.'

Tears splashed down on the twisting fingers and seeing them, Amy flung herself forward across the bed. 'Grandmama,' she cried, using the title for the first time. 'Please, Grandmama.'

The older woman drew herself up, ignoring the pleading touch and imploring eyes of the girl. 'You will leave Kingsclear Court as soon as it can be arranged,' she said with finality. 'If you have any feelings for me at all you will leave this room without further scenes ... and seek fresh adventures elsewhere.'

CHAPTER TEN

Amy spent the rest of the night in her own bedroom, staring out at the dark, storm-filled sky with unseeing eyes, while she faced her suddenly bleak future—a future which held very little of what she had ever hoped for. Finding, as she believed, her own family had not held the happiness she had imagined it would. Sitting in that luxurious chamber in the huge house, she felt more alone and uncared for than she had ever felt at the orphanage.

Morning found her dry eyed and resolute. During the long night she had made her own decision about the future, she would return to Portsmouth and take up her old calling at the orphanage, or if that were not possible, she would ask them to take her in until she could find a position as governess somewhere.

Unable to face a meeting with any of the inmates of the Court, she kept to her room, but was aware of movements and excitement in the house beyond her door. Her meals were brought to her regularly, but until late afternoon no one of the family attempted to see her. Just as the shadows were lengthening Lyddie tapped at the door and begged to be admitted.

Amy opened the door and then went back to her post by the window, staring down at the debris left in the aftermath of the gale.

Lyddie hesitated, before crossing the floor to lay a hand on the other girl's shoulder. 'I would have come sooner, but Grandmama needed me,' she said simply.

'How is she?'

'Tired, but otherwise she has taken no hurt. The doctor came this morning and has left some medicine. And you—?'

Amy sighed and rubbed her hot forehead. 'I have the headache.'

''Tis not surprising, if you have been shut in here all day—come down to the garden with me. The green walk will be private at this hour. I have a message for you from Grandmama.'

As Amy looked at her with sudden hope in her eyes, the other shook her head as she took a pelise out of the clothes press and held it for her. 'The wind is cold,' she said, 'but 'twill serve to blow away your megrims.'

The ground was cold and damp under foot, but the fresh wind was cool and refreshing against Amy's burning cheeks. Looking about at the windblown plants, tumbled arbours and snapped branches lying at their feet, she reflected bitterly that the summer seemed to have flown with her own happiness and, hugging her arms about her chest, she bent into the breeze and walked on.

194

'Shall we sit here?' Lyddie asked, touching her arm and Amy suddenly realised that they had entered the ruins of the nunnery. In the sheltered space the wind had dropped and they could sit quite comfortably on one of the seats tucked under an ivy-clad wall.

'What have you to tell me?' Amy asked, after the silence had grown between them.

'I—am afraid that Lady Kingsclear is still of the same mind.' Lyddie said uncomfortably, her eyes anxious and almost pleading as she looked at the girl beside her. 'We—I pleaded with her but she is adamant and, perhaps it might be best, until the matter h-has blown over, that you should go away.'

Amy shivered and stared at a beetle crossing a flagstone by her feet, but said nothing, waiting for her companion to enlarge upon her theme.

'She has—no wish to be unkind and has sent a letter to our old governess Miss Dill in London, to beg that you may stay with her. You remember I told you that she was the dearest creature? She will take you around and act as your Duenna until someone can be arranged to take you into society.'

'How handsome!'

Wincing at the bitterness in the other's voice, Lydia hurried on. 'Indeed, you will almost have your own establishment. I'd give my fortune to be so free.'

Amy stood up, shaking out her skirts, before

turning to answer. 'Pray thank Lady Kingsclear and say all that is right and proper—you'd manage it so much better than I. Tell her that I want none of her charity.' She stepped carefully over the travelling beetle and stood looking out across the parkland. 'I came in search of my family, but I wish very much that I had not ... my dreams were better than the reality. My father did a wise thing when he left here. Make it clear to your grandmother that I intend to do the same.'

'Amy. You cannot!' Lyddie caught her arm. 'You can't leave here in such a manner. Grandmama would never allow it.'

Amy's thin eyebrows rose. 'No? Pray tell how she will stop me? I hardly think she would lock me in my room.'

'She very well might,' answered Lyddie seriously, 'but only think how could you possibly leave here? My grandmother has only to give the order to the servants and none will drive you. You can hardly walk such a distance as that to the nearest town.'

A thoughtful brown stare passed over her as Amy reviewed the situation and outwardly seemed to aquiesce, but privately she was determined upon her course of action.

Immediately upon her return to the house, she was aware that someone had been in her room, but believing that the servants had taken the opportunity her absence provided to clean the chamber, thought very little of it, until a message from Captain Pensford desired her presence in the library and, entering the book-lined room, she noticed at once that the wooden box which held her Bible was opened upon the table in front of the soldier.

'Why have you taken my box?' she demanded imperiously, walking towards him. 'What right have you to come to my room?'

He looked at her closely, but did not answer her questions. Instead, he pointed to the inlaid box. 'This has belonged to you—for how long?'

'What does it matter?'

'I would be obliged if you would answer my question.'

Amy sighed and shrugged her shoulders elaborately. 'I don't know how long—as long as I can remember.'

'So—it might have belonged to your parents?'

Suddenly she was still. 'I—suppose so.'

'And during that time you have never felt called upon to examine it closely?'

'What do you mean?' She came closer to the table and looked down at the familiar decorated lid, touching it with one finger as she recalled the soldier had done on the day she had shown him her Bible. 'Of course I've looked at it—played with it. I even used to pretend that there was a secret hidy hole in it and that I'd find a clue to my—' Suddenly she broke off and stared up at him. 'Surely you didn't—there isn't—'

'But there is, Miss Clear,' Ellis told her gently. 'When I first saw this box, I knew that I'd seen it, or its counterpart, somewhere before. Last night I saw it in my aunt's room and recalled that there was a secret catch in the lid, where something flat and small, a paper say, could be hidden away.'

Amy's breath was coming quickly and unevenly, her eyes wide with anticipation, were fixed upon the man before her as one clenched hand was pressed hard against the high bodice of her dress.

'Aunt Charlie told me that once she had had a pair, but long ago had given one to Miss Berridge, the vicar's daughter.'

'W-what did you find?' the girl asked hoarsely.

'Your parent's marriage lines,' Ellis told her briefly and put out a steadying hand as she swayed slightly.

Recovering almost at once, she refused his help and, holding tightly to the edge of the table, stared down at the heavily creased oblong of paper that he spread out before her. 'Aubrey William St John Kingsclear,' she read, 'to Charlotte Elizabeth Berridge,' and putting back her head, she sighed deeply, and was silent for a while. 'Charlotte,' she said suddenly. 'You see it was my *mother's* signature in the Bible, not Lady Kingsclear's.'

'Sit down,' advised Ellis Pensford, who had

been watching her closely, 'and let me procure you a glass of brandy.' Ignoring her protests, he placed her in a chair and held a small glass to her lips. Not until she had obediently sipped the fiery liquid was it removed. Reaching out she touched the paper and drew it towards her, reading the crabbed writing with hungry eyes, holding it as if she could not bear to be parted from it.

'It makes a difference,' said Ellis.

'Does it?' she looked up to find him watching her with an expression hard to define in his pale eyes.

'Of course. Now you are an heiress.'

A quick breath and the girl grew very still. 'So—I am,' she breathed and thought quietly for a few minutes, before bending her head to hide her own expression, she asked in a carefully schooled voice, if it made any difference to her grandmother's feelings.

'I am afraid not—but in a while, when she has recovered, *then* she will want to see you.' His voice was unwantedly gentle as he looked down at her. 'An you remember, I told you that Lady Kingsclear had not a great strength of mind. She hides from trials and difficulties ... shortly I am persuaded that her fondness for you will reassert itself and then she will send for you—and you, I hope ... and believe, will have sufficient strength and kindness to forgive her for the pain she has given you and only recall the many kindnesses she has done you.'

Amy looked up to return his glance steadily. 'I didn't do it,' she said simply.

'I know you did not,' he returned.

'And yet you would all have me leave here, rather than say outright that someone else must be guilty? Why must I take the blame? I'm a Kingsclear too, and yet you all band together into a tight little circle and shut me out, while you protect each other.'

Ellis stood near her chair, but did not touch her. 'Once, I asked permission to give you my protection,' he reminded her quietly.

'You didn't mean it,' she cried rather wildly. 'You were making fun of me, or playing some game of your own devising!'

'I'll admit that I had a reason—'

'And now that I am an heiress, you try again!' Aghast at what she had said, she put a hand to her mouth and knew that he would never forget the accusation behind her rash words.

'An you cared to enquire into my affairs, Miss Clear, you would find that, while not as rich as some, I have all I require and have no need to hang out for a fortune as well as a wife.'

With an impeccable bow and the curtest of ice-cold smiles, he was gone, leaving her alone with only her thoughts for company and the realisation that she had just put beyond reach the very thing which she desired most in the world. Slowly, almost imperceptibly, she allowed herself to admit that she loved Ellis

Pensford.

Hearing his voice in the hall as he took his coat and hat from Wilkins, sent her scrambling to her feet in the hope that she could catch him before he left the Court. Snatching up her box and the precious scrap of paper, she ran out of the room, reaching the hall just as the heavy front door closed behind the soldier.

'Mr Ellis?' she asked wildly.

'Has just left, miss,' supplied the butler, looking at her curiously. 'Shall I send a footman after him?'

She hesitated and sighed, clutching her possessions tighter. 'No—no, it doesn't matter,' she said dully and started up the stairs, just as Denvil began to descend.

'I say, was that Ellis?' he asked as they drew level. 'Was there ever such a fellow—I wanted to see him, but he's been closeted first with Lydia, then with Grandmama and now he's gone—'

Amy looked at him thoughtfully, suddenly seeing the answer to her most pressing desires. 'Denvil—an you are not busy, I would have a word with you.'

'Of course,' he replied instantly and turned an inquiring ear.

'Not here—somewhere private.'

Looking a little surprised, he proffered his arm and led her back to the library, closing the door carefully before turning patiently towards her.

The story was easier to tell than she had supposed possible and Denvil proved a good listener, putting in pertinent questions until he had the whole.

'So, you are—a Kingsclear,' he said at last and taking her hand carried it to his lips. 'Welcome, cousin,' he said, pleasing her with the simplicity of his action and making her feel more kindly towards him than she had since his proposal.

'You have told me the story, but I fancy that there is more to it than that.'

'I would leave here—' she said impulsively.

'Leave here!' surprise sounded in his voice and he looked at her with narrowed blue eyes before glancing quickly away.

'Will you help me?' Amy asked. 'I can think of no one else. I wish to go back to Portsmouth and cannot think how to get there, but you—you could procure a carriage and arrange for it to wait at the gate, while I could do none of these things.'

For a moment his gaze was reflective as he looked at the girl thoughtfully, before he smiled and closed his other hand about the fingers he already held. 'My dear cousin, I will do all that is in my power to help you, you may depend. Does my grandmother know of this plan of yours?'

'Of course not—no one does. Lady Kingsclear wants to send me to London as a kind of privileged prisoner to wait until she

202

feels the need to see me—'

'I can understand that such an arrangement is not to your liking,' Denvil assured her, 'but what of Lydia ... and Ellis?'

'Lyddie agrees with her grandmother, in fact she seems to quite like the idea and Ellis...' Unable to find words, she shrugged eloquently and Denvil smiled sympathetically.

'Please,' she said, turning the full force of her pleading eyes upon him. 'Please, Denvil ... You may be sure that I will be grateful.' And with her words she recalled unwillingly that Ellis had once told her that gratitude was a poor thing.

Denvil appeared to hesitate before making up his mind. 'Very well. Cousin Amy,' he said at last. 'I will do it, but not a word to anyone, mind. I'll send a note to the inn at Alford and see what can be arranged.' Looking down at her, he patted her hand encouragingly. 'I'll let you know as soon as maybe, in the meantime, pack your bags, cousin and hold yourself in readiness.'

Amy took his advice and returned to her room, locking the door as she set about deciding which of her wardrobe to take with her. At first she had thought to take only the clothes she had brought with her when she arrived at the Court, but a search revealing no sign of them, she decided with some relief, that they must have been thrown away and contented herself by packing only the most serviceable of her new gowns.

With her carpet bag safely packed and hidden under her bed, she ate her dinner and listened to the familiar sounds as the household prepared itself for sleep. The tall clock in the hall had just struck half of eleven, when a sound drew her eyes to the door as a slip of paper appeared in the crack underneath it.

Snatching it up, she quickly scanned the faintly pencilled words. 'Tomorrow at six of the clock', and blessing Denvil and his efforts on her behalf, she climbed into bed and, despite her excitement, was soon asleep.

The next day passed in a fever of anticipation and half hopes that Ellis might communicate with her, but at last it was over. She had let it be known that she suffered from a headache and no one had been surprised when she kept to her darkened room. Sometime before the appointed hour, she crept down the back stairs, stole around the edge of the house, careful to keep out of sight of the windows, hardly daring to breathe until she was on the drive, safely hidden by the tall, surrounding trees.

Somewhat to her dismay, the road beyond the gate was empty and, taking up as inconspicuous place under that wall as possible, she set her bag at her feet and composed herself to wait. She had not been there more than a few minutes when a stealthy rustling among the trees and bushes that edged the park made her stare about nervously. Suddenly, two grimy hands appeared on the top of the ivy-clad wall, followed by a dirty face, which broke into a wide grin at sight of her.

''Lo, miss,' cried Jem, as one welcoming an old friend. 'I thought I saw you awalking in the park.'

'What are you doing here?' hissed Amy.

The boy swung a leg over the wall and settled himself comfortably. 'Sam and I are pals,' he announced simply.

'The—boy from the lodge?' Amy hazarded a guess.

''Sright, miss. He's teaching me how to rabbit.'

'Indeed ... well, Jem, I'm rather busy. Run along like a good boy.'

Jem was puzzled. 'I thought as you'd like to see me,' he said plaintively. 'The Captain's a swell stable. He keeps the best horse-flesh as I've ever seen and I've lived in towns, you know. The head groom says as I've good hands—he'll teach me to ride.'

'I'm glad you like it there—I'm sure you'll be very happy as long as you're good and work hard.'

'Where you going, miss?' Jem demanded, seeing the bag at her feet. 'Does the Captain know? You're not arunning orf with 'im, are you?'

'No, I am not!' said the girl crossly. 'How

dare you think such a thing—I'm waiting for a coach to take me to Portsmouth, but you are not to tell anyone.'

Solemnly licking a finger and drawing it across his throat with a suitably gruesome gesture the boy gave his promise but seemed annoyed that she'd rejected his idol. 'The Captain's a bang up cove,' he muttered, 'better than that stick o' candle grease any day.'

'You are not to talk of Mr Martin like that,' interposed Amy and was instantly annoyed with herself for having recognised Denvil from the child's graphic, but unflattering description. 'Now, do go away quickly, for here is my coach—I can hear it coming. Goodbye and be a good boy.' Reaching up, she dropped one of her precious store of coins into his eager hand and stepped out from the sheltering wall as a small black coach rumbled round a bend in the road.

At sight of her, the man on the box, shouted to his team and pulled on the reins. 'This Kingsclear Court?' he demanded.

'Yes, yes, do be quick,' cried Amy in a fever to be gone before someone arrived to stop her escape.

With irritating slowness the man climbed down and, opening the door helped her into the dim interior, tossing in her bag with scant regard for its contents. So eager was she to be away from the Court, that the horses were in full stride before Amy realised that she was not alone. A gentleman leaned back in the corner of the seat opposite, regarding her astonishment with a slight smile.

'Denvil!' she exclaimed. 'What do you here?'

'I thought to accompany you for a little. I would never forgive myself if any harm befell you on your journey.'

'Pooh, what could happen to me?' Amy said roundly. 'I intend to put up at the hostel in Leahook for the night.'

'You don't consider that cousin Ellis might follow?'

Amy was still, almost holding her breath. 'W-why should he? I am sure that Captain Pensford will be glad to see the back of me.'

'Perhaps. When you were merely an orphanage miss, almost certainly, but now that you are an heiress, I fancy the matter may be viewed in a different light.'

'But why?'

'The Kingsclears like to keep a hold on their wealth.'

A note of bitterness in his low voice made her glance swiftly at him, but he met her look with a bland smile, searching inside his coat for a gold watch at which he glanced before returning it to his pocket.

'Doubtless dinner is being served at the Court,' said Amy following his gaze. 'Won't they wonder at your absence?'

'Not they—I am dining with friends, for I took the care to make my plans known before I left this morning. I took the liberty to believe that you would care for a companion on your journey.'

'I am no fainting female, sir.'

'But I am persuaded that any lady of tender susceptibilities would feel the need of a gentleman's presence. Tobymen abound on these heaths, you know and even such as you would not be free from their attentions, should they decide to hold up the coach. I had to pay the Jarveyman double the usual amount before he would agree to hire himself and his vehicle to me.'

'I am very grateful,' Amy felt constrained to say a little stiffly.

'No need, I assure you, cousin. My devotion is yours—anything you have a care for, I would do all in my power to provide.'

Taking off his hat and laying it on the seat beside him, he leaned forward. Amy drew back, a faint elusive perfume wafting towards her. Wrinkling her nose at the familiar scent, she tried to recall where she had smelt it before and the memory returned to her with startling abruptness.

'It was you!' she cried before she could stop herself.

Narrow blue eyes regarded her across the confines of the coach and from his sudden tense stillness, she knew that he was aware of her knowledge. Running a hand across his carefully ordered hair, he smiled ruefully.

'I really had no idea that my hairdressing was so distinctive. You smelt it on the sheet, of course.'

'How could you? Poor Lady Kingsclear—your own grandmother.'

He shrugged. 'She took no hurt,' he said, a note of indifference in his voice.

'But why? Do you dislike me so much?'

'No. In fact had you not been a danger to the amount which Lady Kingsclear would leave me and to which I could persuade a banker to finance me, I would have quite liked you.'

Fascinated by his duplicity, Amy stared at him, making no attempt to hide the scorn she felt and even in the dim evening light, could see the faint tinge that coloured his cheeks.

'I should have been warned,' she said clearly. 'I've a fancy that Lyddie has your measure.'

He laughed. 'Ellis, too. He's bailed me out a few times and even warned me off you once or twice—though I've a notion that it was you he was interested in even then. You, or rather your money, my dear.'

'I had no money.'

'No—but the distinct possibility of acquiring some. Lack of money is the curse of mankind. We should all be as rich as Croesus. I had a gambling father, Amy and all he had to leave me when he died were debts—and a family liking for gambling.'

'You have my condolences,' Amy told him dryly. 'You had an education and a position.

Could you not have done something with them? Many before you have.'

'Lord! Can you see me as a penniless tutor to some merchant's dullard son? I was born a gentleman and could not be expected to earn my living.'

'But, you could try to drown me.'

He had the grace to look a little uncomfortable. 'That, I assure you, went too far—I intended only to frighten you into leaving the Court. I was near at hand ... and had no idea that you would get so far out, on the lake before the punt sank.'

'How relieved you must have been when Ellis rode by.' Amy eyed him thoughtfully. 'It was you, of course, with the gipsy that morning and I suppose that you shut me in the ruins, when I first arrived.'

'That, I can't claim—I imagine it was either Medora or the wind.'

'But of course it was you that tore out the page of the register at the Church at Alford.'

'It was in the pocket of my jacket that day when I found you sitting on the stile in the lane,' he agreed.

'What did it say?' she asked curiously.

'What you hoped it would ... that your parents had been married there.'

'You destroyed it?'

'Of course.'

She sighed. 'I should have liked to see it. How annoyed you must have been when I told you that the certificate had been found and shown to Lady Kingsclear.'

'I had to review my plans, certainly.'

'What a pity that all your scheming has come to nought.'

A silent laugh shook him and a gleam of triumph in his eyes made Amy grow uneasy. Something made her glance out of the window, gazing at the unfamiliar countryside with troubled eyes. For a while the coach lumbered on, lurching along the dusty road, pock-marked by the winter rains and rutted by the wheels of other vehicles. A signpost appeared, leaning drunkenly against the hedge and for a moment Amy stared at it uncomprehendingly, before turning on her companion with wide, accusing eyes.

'Reading!' she cried. 'That signpost was pointing to Reading. Stop this coach at once. We are going the wrong way.'

'Compose yourself, cousin,' Denvil said, leaning forward to take her hands, when she would have tapped on the Jarvey's window above the seat. 'I told you that I was forced to review my plans, remember. My apologies, but I quite forgot to inform you that going to Portsmouth was not among them.'

Slowly she subsided, unable to free her hands and gazed at him, with puzzled eyes. 'Do you intend to abduct me?' she asked frankly. 'I truly cannot imagine Lady Kingsclear paying a ransom.'

'Nothing of the kind,' he told her, 'but I will confess to a long held wish to visit Scotland. I believe it is considered particularly beautiful at this time of the year. Not, of course, that we need go far—just across the border in fact.' He saw by her expression that she understood and carried her hands to his lips. 'You have my promise to make you a goodly husband,' he said and kissed the backs of her hands.

'I have no intention of marrying you, sir,' she cried, snatching her hands away. 'Nothing you could say would persuade me to such an action.'

'Then I am afraid that you will be quite ruined—not even the prospect of your wealth would find you a respectable husband once it is known that you went to Gretna Green with me. It might even be news abroad that you did Ellis a similar kindness—'

'You revolt me!'

Denvil looked at her bright eyes and heightened colour with dislike. 'You would do well to curb your temper—I find that I do not care for a termagant to wife.'

At that moment the shrill note of a horn demanding passageway was heard and Amy looked at her companion with startled hope in her eyes. Leaning out of the window, she had time to see the familiar greys draw level, followed by Ellis driving his curricle. Nodding deliberately to the inmates of the coach, his eyes found hers, briefly before he was past, leaving an impression of flying coat capes and the grinning face of his tiger as he waved his yard-of-tin deprecatingly.

'What now, Denvil?' Amy asked softly, setting back into her corner of the coach with a quiet air of triumph.

For answer the man tapped on the window above his head and demanded that the driver turn off the road.

'Can't be done,' came the stolid reply. 'For there isn't such a thing from here to Hemworth.'

Fuming Denvil sank down, his chin in his cravat and Amy shot him a dancing glance.

'He'll be waiting for us,' she told him. 'Perhaps it would be wise for you to leave me—'

'Whatever you may think, I am not afraid to face my cousin,' he said to her surprise and a tense silence developed between them as the coach drew inexorably towards the large, sprawling village of Hemworth.

'Draw in at the inn,' Denvil called to the driver as they reached the outskirts and, peering from the window, Amy saw Ellis's greys already being led towards the stables of the red brick inn.

As Denvil turned to give Amy his hand as she climbed down from the coach, a beaming landlord appeared in the wide doorway.

'Come in, come in,' he smiled, bowing profusely. 'Captain Pensford has ordered dinner and it will be set upon the table in a few minutes.'

Rather bemused, Amy followed him into the interior of the building and allowed herself to be led into a low-ceilinged room, with an uneven floor. At their entrance, the gentleman by the newly lit fire turned and sketched a bow.

'As you can see, I arrived first,' said Ellis and taking Amy's hand in a comforting grasp, led her towards the fire, 'and took it upon myself to order a meal for us all. I have explained, cousin Amy, how it is that we were to meet here and that now I shall escort you home—how is your poor maid? Not still suffering the agonies of toothache, I hope?'

Amy blinked, but quickly recovered her wits and followed, with tolerable ease, the lead presented to her. 'Bessie, poor soul, is lying upon a bed of pain, I'm afraid ... I left her with my aunt and arranged that she will follow when she had had the tooth pulled.'

'Very wise,' said Ellis gravely, 'especially as your journey was so important.' He turned to the landlord, who had listened to this exchange with lively interest, 'Miss Clear comes to nurse my ... sister.'

'My condolences, sir,' offered the other man affably, preparing to bring in the meal his wife had organised. 'There's a thick soup and a cold pie as well as a smoked ham,' he explained, 'with salmon as a side dish with a little salad.'

'It sounds delightful,' put in Amy, drawing

214

off her gloves and untying her bonnet strings.

'Shall I see about bedchambers?' asked the landlord hopefully, casting a last glance at the laden table.

'I think that none of us will require rooms,' said Ellis suavely. 'In fact Mr Martin will be leaving directly after dinner.'

Denvil shot him a resentful glance, but said nothing until the landlord had withdrawn. 'It's all very well for you, Ellis,' he said a little pettishly, 'to make arrangements, but the night draws on and soon it will be dark. Do you expect me to cross the heath by moonlight?'

Ellis looked steadily across the table, toying with a wineglass with one long, brown hand. Amy watched the red liquor swirling round and reflecting the points of light from the candles and, when he spoke, started a little.

'Your activities hold little interest for me,' the soldier said quietly. 'So long as they take place at the greatest possible distance.'

Denvil, who had been leaning back, sipping his own drink with every sign of ease, abruptly sat up and set down his glass with a sudden snap. 'An I mistake me not, cousin, that has all the sounds of a threat,' he observed slowly.

'You make no mistake.'

At the familiar hint of menace in his voice, Amy's eyes flew to his face and she found that his grey eyes were cold and glinting with an air of danger. Leaning back in his chair, apparently at ease, his shoulders were taut and

215

she knew that his every nerve was tight with tension. Catching her own breath, she glanced at Denvil and saw that he understood his cousin very well.

With a deprecating laugh, the younger man deliberately took up his glass again and swallowed the contents with a quick flick of his wrist. 'Understand, Ellis,' he said, his voice not quite steady, 'that I have no desire to quarrel with you.'

'That, Denvil, is all to the well ... but strangely disappointing,' murmured the other.

Denvil spread his hands. 'Think you that I have forgotten what happened when last we fought?'

'I've a mind that I won—'

'As ever, your memory is quite right. I would tell you plainly that I have never bet on a sure thing. And I believe that if we fought tonight, you have every intention of winning and not holding your arm ... even though I am a kinsman.'

'How astute,' smiled Ellis blandly, his eyes as cold as ice and Amy shivered a little as he went on, his voice clear and almost devoid of feeling. 'What a pity that you were not always so far-sighted. Did you really believe that you could blacken Amy's name so that Aunt Charlie sent her away for ever ... or did you think that murder was an easier alternative?'

'Never that, Ellis ... the accident at the lake went further than I intended.'

216

'Luckily, I believe you. Although you've ever been spoiled and foolish, I've never known you totally cruel before, even to get your own way. I conclude that your debts have mounted until you faced ruin and that such disaster was more than you could stand. When Amy appeared and you understood that she might stand between you and Aunt Charlie's money, you lost your head and turned to rash acts, which normally you would never have considered.'

'How well you put it,' murmured the other. 'You understand me almost better than I do myself.'

For a moment the cousins faced each other across the table and something of the tension between them left the room.

'What now, Ellis?' breathed Denvil after a pause. 'Will you tell Grandmama and the girls?'

'Lady Kingsclear must know something of the whole—as to what she tells Lydia and Medora, that will be her decision ... as long as you leave the country.'

The fragile stem of the glass snapped under Denvil's fingers and he carefully laid it aside, wiping his hand before he spoke. 'Leave the country?'

'A packet leaves Southampton harbour for America tomorrow. An you are on it, I shall make a sum of money payable to you at a New York bank.'

217

'And if not?'

Ellis shrugged. 'You really have little choice, you know,' he said almost conversationally. 'If you stay here, you only face a future of growing debts and misery, for you may be sure that I shall not be liable for any of your bills and that I shall make certain that you don't play upon your grandmother's susceptibilities. Think about it, Denvil . . . the sum I mentioned would be—considerable.'

'And what would stop me from taking the money and the first ship home?'

The smile that curved Ellis's mouth was not nice. 'Your own good sense, cousin,' he said softly and as Denvil's eyes fell, Amy knew that he had won and so, apparently, did Ellis for he turned away from his cousin and payed attention to the neglected meal.

Denvil played with the food on his plate, making a pretence of eating, glancing now and again across at the other man. 'Tell me,' he said suddenly, 'I am curious as to how you found us on the road so quickly. I had supposed that we had at least the night clear before you would find our trail.'

'Jem is proving useful. I am afraid that he took a dislike to you, Denvil, and when he saw you in the coach with Amy and it turned in the wrong direction for Portsmouth, he was only too keen to seek me out and make the matter known to me.'

Denvil's laugh was rueful as he stood up and

threw down his napkin. 'I can think of nothing more that must be said between us,' he said. 'I will leave you ... and trust that you will make my excuses to Lady Kingsclear.' Turning to Amy, he bowed elegantly, his fair hair shining in the glow of the candles. 'I should make my apologies to you, cousin, but I have a feeling that your future is more settled than mine.' His eyes flickered from her to Ellis and a tight smile played about his mouth as he straightened his shoulders. 'I find that the prospect of visiting our American colonies vaguely pleasing,' he admitted. 'You may be surprised to find that I am of pioneering stuff.'

There was a silence after he had gone and then Ellis reached across and refilled Amy's glass.

'To the American branch of our family,' he said and drained his glass.

'I would like to see you suffer a set down,' said the girl. 'You arrange everything so well and are so satisfied by your efforts that you don't think of the effect upon other people.'

One black eyebrow rose into a peak. 'You'll forgive me for thinking that I managed that rather well ... or have I mistaken the matter and you would have preferred to reach Gretna Green undetected?'

'Of course not! I have no wish to marry your cousin. In fact I found him irritating in the extreme. He told me that he had no wish for a termagant for a wife!'

'Hardly conducive to a happy matrimonial life,' agreed Ellis.

'He only wanted my money.'

'I am sure he found your other . . . attractions equally desirable.'

Amy stiffened and sent him an indignant glance. 'You are teasing,' she accused.

'Indeed, I am,' said Ellis, 'but allow me to say that I find your attractions eminently more desirable than your fortune. For sometime I have known the strongest wish to kiss you upon every occasion—even when my hand itched to give you the beating you deserved.'

'Then let me tell you, sir,' the girl began roundly, 'That you have—*What* did you say?'

'That you deserved to feel my hand.'

Ignoring the twinkle in his eyes, she shook her head impatiently. 'No—no. Before that.'

'That I wanted to kiss you,' Ellis repeated, coming round the table and drawing her to her feet.

Amy knew that she should be scandalised, but found that she liked the security of his arms about her and that her face seemed to rise of its own accord to meet his.

The landlord chose that inauspicious moment to enter and withdrew quickly, mouthing an apology and bowing obsequiously. With a smothered oath, Ellis threw some coins on the table and, tucking Amy under his arm, gave her only time to snatch up her reticule and bonnet, before sweeping her out of the inn.

The grey evening dusk had settled round the inn, but yellow light from its windows streamed across the wide road, showing the startled ostlers running to bring out the greys and harness them to the curricle.

'I would liefer not go back to the Court.' Amy said in a low voice. 'At least not for a while.'

'I have an elderly Godmother living a few miles away. Shall we pay her a visit? I am persuaded that she would be pleased to see us—nothing has ever put her out of countenance.' Dancing grey eyes glanced down at her. 'Or . . . we could continue Denvil's journey and travel to Scotland,' he suggested daringly.

Amy smiled steadily up at him. 'An you wish,' she answered with perfect confidence.

'I've not made you a declaration, yet.'

'No,' she agreed and hung her head. 'Perhaps there is time for me to join Denvil.'

His grip around her shoulder tightened. 'Don't trifle with me, orphanage miss,' he told her. 'You know I'd only follow and bring you back.'

She sighed. 'Then—Scotland it had better be.'

The carriage had arrived and without waiting for the steps to be let down, he tossed her up into the seat. The tiger made to climb up behind, but catching his master's eye, he grinned and, touching his cap, slid back into the shadows of the buildings behind.

'We'll be ostracised,' Ellis warned as the horses jerked into motion.

'I daresay,' Amy agreed. 'The brave Captain Pensford carrying off an unknown foundling from an orphanage will serve as gossip for weeks.' She turned an artless face to her companion. 'Will you cast me off when you grow tired of me?'

The soldier ground his teeth. 'You know full well I intend to marry you,' he said. 'Vixen! I believe that you had designs on me all the time and inveigled me into your clutches with feminine cunning from the beginning.'

'No,' Amy told him frankly. 'At first I disliked you very much. I thought you arrogant and overbearing.'

'And now?'

'Now I *know* you're overbearing and arrogant . . . and I like you more than I can say.'

'Love,' corrected Ellis firmly, tooling his team round a bend in the narrow dark lane.

'I love you,' repeated Amy obediently and nestled against his side.

One blue covered arm encircled her and suddenly a laugh shook her companion and she glanced up enquiringly.

'I never thought I'd be grateful for that ball that took me in the arm,' he explained, 'but I must say, I own a gladness that I am able to drive with one hand.'

222

And bending his head to find her mouth, Captain Pensford proceeded to demonstrate that not only could he drive single handed, but could find the road with only one eye and less than half his attention.